JACK BE NIMBLE

A Just Jack Thriller

Also by J. Robert Kennedy

James Acton Thrillers

The Protocol
Brass Monkey
Broken Dove
The Templar's Relic
Flags of Sin
The Arab Fall
The Circle of Eight
The Venice Code
Pompeii's Ghosts
Amazon Burning
The Riddle
Blood Relics
Sins of the Titanic
Saint Peter's Soldiers
The Thirteenth Legion
Raging Sun
Wages of Sin
Wrath of the Gods
The Templar's Revenge
The Nazi's Engineer
Atlantis Lost
The Cylon Curse
The Viking Deception
Keepers of the Lost Ark
The Tomb of Genghis Khan
The Manila Deception
The Fourth Bible
Embassy of the Empire
Armageddon
No Good Deed
The Last Soviet
Lake of Bones
Fatal Reunion
The Resurrection Tablet
The Antarctica Incident
The Ghosts of Paris
No More Secrets
The Curse of Imhotep
The Sword of Doom

Dylan Kane Thrillers

Rogue Operator
Containment Failure
Cold Warriors
Death to America
Black Widow
The Agenda
Retribution
State Sanctioned
Extraordinary Rendition
Red Eagle
The Messenger
The Defector
The Mole
The Arsenal

Just Jack Thrillers

You Don't Know Jack
Jack Be Nimble

Templar Detective Thrillers

The Templar Detective
The Parisian Adulteress
The Sergeant's Secret
The Unholy Exorcist
The Code Breaker
The Black Scourge
The Lost Children
The Satanic Whisper

Kriminalinspektor Wolfgang Vogel Mysteries

The Colonel's Wife
Sins of the Child

Delta Force Unleashed Thrillers

Payback
Infidels
The Lazarus Moment
Kill Chain
Forgotten
The Cuban Incident
Rampage
Inside the Wire
Charlie Foxtrot
A Price Too High

Detective Shakespeare Mysteries

Depraved Difference
Tick Tock
The Redeemer

Zander Varga, Vampire Detective

The Turned

JACK BE NIMBLE

A Just Jack Thriller

J. ROBERT KENNEDY

UNDERMILL
PRESS

This is a work of fiction. Names, characters, places, and incidents are products of the author's imagination. Any resemblance to actual persons, living or dead, is entirely coincidental.

ISBN: 9781998005536

First Edition

For Matthew Perry.

Can we BE more devastated?

JACK BE NIMBLE

A Just Jack Thriller

"I disapprove of what you say, but I will defend to the death your right to say it."

Voltaire

"The main problem is [Minister of Defense] Shoigu and [Chief of the General Staff] Gerasimov. It was the decisions of those two that blocked us from getting everything, despite the president saying that the ammunition was there."

Yevgeny Prigozhin, Leader of the Wagner Group
May 2023

PREFACE

For approximately 24 hours, starting June 23, 2023, the world watched in shock as the unthinkable unfolded—a Russian rebellion. A private paramilitary organization, funded by Moscow and led by a close ally of Russian President Vladimir Putin, took over the Russian city of Rostov-on-Don without encountering any resistance, despite it being the location of the Southern Military District headquarters.

But that was just the beginning.

Shortly after securing their position, as many as 8,000 mercenaries were sent north toward Moscow, armed with state-of-the-art weaponry, including Russian-supplied anti-aircraft systems, on a mission to arrest the leaders of the Russian military.

As the rebels advanced, they encountered ever-increasing resistance, yet despite this, some reports have them coming within sixty miles of the outskirts of Moscow.

And then they stopped.

The crisis and possible civil war was averted, the remarkable events concluding in a way that surprised most experts. Perhaps if they had known the whole truth, they might not have been.

For an American had played a critical role during this rebellion.

A CIA Operations Officer known as Jack.

Just Jack.

The Front Lines

Ukraine

CIA Operations Officer Sherrie White winced as the scene played out in front of her. She was hidden in underbrush half a mile away, her ghillie suit blending perfectly with the terrain, scarred by over a year of war. She had seen death. She had taken lives. But in her short career, she had never been in a war zone, and had certainly never seen anything like this.

Another shot was fired, then another, as the shooter placed a bullet in each of the Ukrainian soldiers, men fighting to defend their country from an evil aggressor, men who had paid the ultimate price for their family and loved ones.

It was heartbreaking.

It frustrated her to no end that there were naïve morons back home who felt her country shouldn't be helping defend against the brutal Russian attack. But for the moment, she was simply disturbed.

For the man executing the Ukrainians was someone she considered a friend.

A man she knew only as Jack.

Just Jack.

Roof of the Fairfax Towers

Falls Church, Virginia

Three Days Earlier

"What's on your mind?"

CIA Analyst Supervisor Chris Leroux flinched, his thoughts having drifted to the latest briefing notes he had read this morning. He had the weekend off, but a job like his rarely allowed such luxuries. He glanced over at his super-spy girlfriend, Sherrie White. "What's that?"

She rolled her eyes. "Don't tell me you haven't heard a word that's been said."

CIA Operations Officer and Leroux's best friend in the world, Dylan Kane, took a sip of his Thai Singha beer. "He's been gone for at least five minutes. I recognize that glazed-over expression anywhere."

The love of Kane's life, ex-Chinese Special Forces Major Lee Fang, sat up in her lounge chair, revealing her rippling abs, the woman in *ridonculous* good shape. "Is something bothering you?"

Leroux sighed. "Yeah. It's the situation in Belarus."

"Can you talk about it?"

He shrugged. "Sherrie and Dylan are cleared but you're not, though I can talk in broader terms that you've seen on the news."

"What is it, buddy?" asked Kane, placing his beer on the artificial turf laid out on top of their apartment building's roof, an oasis thrown together by the tenants over the years. "Are you referring to the nukes?"

"That's definitely part of it. The biggest part, obviously. It's unprecedented. It's one thing to position nukes on the territory of an ally. We did it for years. But to transfer control and ownership, that's pretty much unheard of, especially from the Russians. Belarus is an insignificant state, a puppet of Moscow. Why would you ever transfer nukes to a country like that? It makes no sense."

Kane agreed. "Yeah, I was thinking the same thing when I heard about it. What possible benefit is there? It's not like they need to buy their loyalty. They already pretty much control that country. The Russian president has his fist so far up the Belarusian leader's ass, he controls his jaw. Anything that man says is dictated by Moscow."

"Exactly. That's why this is so strange. For the life of me, I can't think of a reason for Moscow to do this."

Fang took a sip of her margarita, a pitcher of the ice-cold beverage prepared by Sherrie sitting nearby. "Could it be for money, like that Chinese deal you helped break up?"

Leroux dismissed the idea. "No. That's what I thought at first as well, but the number of warheads are too few, and Belarus doesn't have any money for something like that. And besides, the bigger part of that agreement between Russia and China was the mutual defense pact and the annual payments that would get them through the war and any sanctions. No, this is something entirely different. It's not money. You don't give somebody nukes to get leverage over them, and Russia would never give someone nukes that could then be used as leverage against them. They had to have transferred them for a specific reason."

Sherrie put down her drink. "You mean this is all part of a bigger plan?"

"Yes. It has to be. But if the plan involves nukes, are they a deterrent, a threat, or do they actually intend to use them."

Kane finished off his beer. "A deterrent makes no sense. There's no threat to Belarus. Not from NATO. Even if Belarus decided to get actively involved in the invasion of Ukraine, NATO still wouldn't act. Belarus knows that and Russia knows that. And besides, they have a mutual defense agreement, so there's no reason for Russia to transfer nukes there and give them control."

Sherrie agreed. "That leaves using them as a threat or actually using them. The threat would be an empty one. Nobody would believe that Belarus would use the weapons. The Russians have been threatening for a year now and even they haven't used them. So, any threats would be ignored."

Kane frowned. "Then that leaves actually using them."

"They have to know NATO would react to that."

A sickening pit formed in Leroux's stomach as a thought occurred to him. "That's it. It has to be."

"What do you mean?"

"Russia knows that if they use nukes on the battlefield, they've crossed a line that NATO has to respond to."

Sherrie's jaw dropped. "But if Belarus launched, NATO can't respond against Russia."

"Exactly. They can only respond against the pawn. And by then it'd be too late. Ukraine would be forced to surrender."

Kane stared at him. "That can't be right. That can't be what's going on."

Fang grabbed at her hair. "It can't be. It would lead to the destruction of Belarus. Even if they are a puppet of Moscow, there's no way they'd launch knowing what would happen to them."

Kane rose, wagging a finger. "No, puppets like that do what they're told, and I can guarantee you before they launched, he'd be in Moscow, dining with his master."

Sherrie rose, her face pale. "Nobody is that crazy."

"Oh? You don't think that psycho in Moscow isn't crazy enough to think up something like this?"

"But it's diabolical. Millions could die. Hell, if it got out of control, billions."

"Men like that don't care as long as they're not one of the billions." Kane turned to Leroux. "You have to go to the Chief with this immediately. You need to find out what the hell's going on and some way to stop it."

Leroux frowned. "But how do you stop a nuclear attack when the politicians won't allow you to fire a single shot?"

Director Morrison's Office, CIA Headquarters

Langley, Virginia

National Clandestine Service Chief Leif Morrison leaned back in his chair, his fingers drumming against the top of his desk. Leroux waited for a response to the outlandish theory he and his friends had come up with at the start of what was supposed to be a day of fun in the sun and getting hammered. Morrison was several rungs higher than Leroux at the Agency, but the man had taken him under his wing years ago, recognizing a potential in him that Leroux still wasn't sure he saw himself. He was now the youngest analyst supervisor in history and had earned the respect of those who served him and those he served.

"Sometimes that famous gut of yours terrifies me."

"You and me both."

Morrison regarded him. "Just how many sheets into the wind were you when you came up with this?"

"Second beer, sir. Don't worry."

"Let's make sure your report says you were sipping sodas at the sock hop or something innocent like that."

Leroux smirked. "Sock hop, sir? I think that even predates your youth."

"Then you know it must be innocent. So, your theory—"

"Dylan, Sherrie, and Fang contributed."

"Let's leave the Chinese spy out of your report."

"Of course, sir. And don't worry, nothing classified was discussed. Only things that have already been reported in the news or you could find out on Telegram."

"Good. So, your theory is that the nukes transferred to Belarus by Russia is not part of their mutual defense pact, but is instead part of a plan to actually use the nukes and blame someone other than Russia?"

"Yes, sir."

"Obviously, the plan would be to use them on Ukraine."

"That's our thinking."

"And you originally thought the Belarusians would launch them instead of the Russians, but now you're not so sure?"

"I'm not, sir. The Belarusians have to know we'd respond if they launched. It doesn't make sense for them to put their country at risk."

"So the Russians will make it look like they did, and let them take the blame."

Leroux shrugged. "That's what I was thinking, but I have no evidence to support it."

"I think you have no evidence to support any of it."

Leroux held up his hands. "Unfortunately, you're right. We need someone to start looking into this."

"Who do we have available?"

"Well, sir, Jack is already in Belarus gathering intel on the nuke transfer. It would be fairly easy to retask him."

"Do it. We need to know what the hell's going on and quickly. At the morning briefing, the Pentagon reported large troop movements on the Russian-Belarus border. The Russians are getting ready for something, and I have a funny feeling it's all related. If we don't get a handle on this quickly, we could be in the biggest war since Korea."

Leroux/White Residence, Fairfax Towers

Falls Church, Virginia

"Well, this weekend didn't turn out as planned."

Sherrie's friend, and probably best female friend, Lee Fang, agreed. "No, but that's the nature of the beast when it comes to life in the CIA. At least you're getting to go off and have some fun. I'm stuck here waiting for you guys to come back and entertain me."

Sherrie paused for a moment and regarded her friend. "I'm sorry about how things worked out for you. You know that, right?"

Fang shrugged. "It was this or death. I think I came out on the right side of the equation."

Sherrie chuckled, resuming her inspection of her three-day go bag, this one for northern hemisphere fall weather. "I suppose that's one way of looking at it. Where's Dylan off to?"

"China. I think they want him in theater just in case this nuclear war thing does happen and my former homeland decides to take advantage of it."

"One man, stopping the entire Chinese army from invading Taiwan?"

Fang grinned. "If you asked Dylan, he'd say those odds were pretty even."

Sherrie laughed, zipping up her bag. "Oh, that man has an ego on him, doesn't he?"

"Definitely. In his job, he has to. Which means so do you."

Sherrie stared at her in horror. "You think I have an ego?"

"Nothing like Dylan's, but you've got one." Fang waved her hands. "Don't worry, I don't mind. I have one too. Remember, I was Special Forces. You can't not have one when you know ten different ways to kill a man twice your size with just your thumb."

Sherrie giggled. "I know. It's awesome, isn't it?"

"It is. I just wish I got more chances to use what I know."

Sherrie sat on the edge of the bed. "It is exciting, going out and saving the world or some small part of it, but the fact it's necessary is ridiculous. It's the modern age. Why the hell can't we just get along? You think about the world today, and it's a horrible place. Even here. This isn't my America."

"I blame social media. The fact your country hasn't banned TikTok is simply flabbergasting. Frankly, I'd ban all social media. It would solve more problems than it would create."

Sherrie rose, grabbing her bag. "You're preaching to the choir." She struck a pose. "So, how do I look?"

Fang gave her the once over. "I'd switch."

Sherrie grinned. "That's what I want to hear." She headed for the door. "Now to go help a man with an ego possibly bigger than Dylan's, and definitely bigger than mine."

East of Mogilev, Belarus

CIA Operations Officer Jack—just Jack—peered through his binoculars from the comfort of an SUV supplied by Minsk Station. He had been in Belarus for a week now, observing the transfer of Russian nuclear weapons to this puppet regime, and frowned as yet more made their way into the former Soviet Republic.

He could understand why Washington was concerned. The move was unprecedented. Nuclear weapons stationed on an ally's soil were commonplace. The United States had been doing it for decades.

But this was different.

This was the transfer of operational control. It meant the Belarusians could launch the weapons themselves. When America stationed its nukes on foreign soil, those weapons were always under the command and control of Washington. No foreign power could ever launch them. It was American soldiers crewing the systems, and American commanders issuing the launch orders.

But not here.

Here, the Russians, for some inexplicable reason, were handing that control over. It made no sense, which was one of the reasons he had been sent in. Track the weapons, and attempt to determine why this insanity was taking place.

His comms, buried deep in his ear canal, squawked. "Jackrabbit, Control Actual. Come in, over."

Jack cocked an eyebrow at Chris Leroux's voice. David Epps had been his Control so far on this mission. For Leroux to identify himself as Control Actual meant something was going on, and his mission was likely about to change. "This is Jackrabbit, go ahead, over."

"Jackrabbit, as of now, I will be taking over as Control for your mission. We have a situation that we need you to look into, and since it's my theory, I'm stuck with you."

Jack chuckled. He liked Leroux. He had a good sense of humor, and the hottest girlfriend in the business. "I love you too, Control. What's the situation?"

"We might have come up with a plausible scenario as to why Russia is transferring those nukes."

This piqued Jack's interest. "Oh?"

"We believe they intend to launch the nukes against Ukraine, and blame Belarus. That way we can't retaliate against Russia, and Ukraine falls."

Jack whistled. It was a crazy idea, but then again, the world had gone crazy. It made sense, though there was a flaw. "Sounds insane, so exactly what I'd expect to come out of Moscow. One problem, though."

"What's that?"

"I can't believe the Belarusians would agree to it. They have to know they'd get the shit hammered out of them if they launched."

"That's our thinking as well. It's why we think they might not know the plan."

Jack pursed his lips, thinking for a moment. "If the Russians intend to launch the missiles themselves, from Belarusian territory, then that means they intend to make it look like the Belarusians did it. Moscow might be stupid enough to believe they might get away with it, but I think there has to be at least one brain over there that might point that out."

"What are you thinking?"

"I'm not sure, but I have an idea."

"What?"

"Best I don't say this over the airwaves. I'll send you a secure message with my thoughts. I'm going to need some help, however."

"Skylark is already on her way."

Jack smiled. "Can't wait. What's our cover?"

"*Not* boyfriend and girlfriend."

Jack groaned for Leroux's benefit. "Dude, you're no fun."

Forward Operating Base Echo 62

Ukrainian-Controlled Territory, Ukraine

"It's disrespectful!"

CIA Operations Officer Jack—just Jack—understood the Ukrainian commander's sentiments. What he was proposing was almost unthinkable. Yet it had to be done. If he couldn't convince the man, this plan was dead in the water. He stepped closer, softening his tone slightly. "I understand how you feel, but think of it this way. It gives these fallen heroes one more chance to contribute to the cause. All these men will have already died honorably fighting for their country. I'm not asking for anyone else to die. And you know they'd volunteer if they knew what was at stake."

Colonel Kovalenko closed his eyes, squeezing his temples. "How certain are you?"

Jack shrugged. "Not at all, unfortunately. But the person who came up with this scenario is someone I trust implicitly, and even if there's a one in a million chance it's true, don't you agree we have to do everything we can to stop it?"

Kovalenko sighed and stared at him. "I just wish we knew for sure."

"That's the whole point of this. One last ask of six of your men who've already paid the ultimate price could save the lives of millions."

Kovalenko's jaw squared as he drew a deep breath, steeling himself. "I can't believe I'm agreeing to this, but you're right. If there's even the remotest chance, we have to do everything we can to stop it. Otherwise, this war is lost."

Disputed Territory

West of Bakhmut, Ukraine

Jack fired a round into the chest of one of the Ukrainians, the body shaking from the impact, but there was no other reaction, nor would there be. He moved to the second Ukrainian, firing again, the shot ringing out over the still of a temporary lull in the battle, coordinated with the Ukrainian regional command.

The shots had to be heard.

He was only a couple of miles from the front lines of this particular area controlled by a Russian mercenary group known to the world as Valkyrie. The entire aim here was to gain their attention and have them investigate.

He fired again, the corpse barely moving from the kinetic energy. Six men, all killed on the front lines within the past 24 hours, provided by their commander for one last heroic sacrifice, a staged massacre that would hopefully impress Valkyrie.

He fired a round into the final body, the scene set. A light armored vehicle was parked on the side of the road, six bodies surrounding it, strewn about and shot. It didn't appear staged. Not at first glance, but if anyone were to examine the scene, they would quickly discover the subterfuge. The wounds weren't fresh, and those delivered by him didn't bleed, for there was no functioning heart to pump the blood. It was why the next phase of the operation was critical.

An engine roared behind him and he turned to see several Russian light armored vehicles racing toward him, Valkyrie flags flying from the rear. This was it. He holstered his sidearm and swung his AK-47 into a resting position, just in case things turned ugly. There was no way in hell he would survive if these new arrivals didn't fall for his trickery, but he would at least have a chance to take some of them out.

The vehicles skidded to a halt, the doors opening, over a dozen men stepping out, their weapons raised.

"What the hell happened here?" asked a major.

The fact they hadn't opened fire at him was a good sign. Jack shrugged. "We had a disagreement."

"What kind of disagreement?"

"They asked who I was. I didn't feel like telling them. Then one thing led to another."

The new arrivals spread out, covering him, but also taking in the scene. He couldn't risk them having too much time to find the problems. He reached out and pulled a patch off the shoulder of one of the downed men. He tossed it to the major. "Check their insignia. Special Forces."

"Major, look at this!" A Valkyrie corporal pulled something from one of the victim's hands and held it up. "It's a photo of the general, sir."

Jack jerked his chin toward the photo he had planted only moments ago. "Looks like they were coming for your boss."

The major took the photo and frowned. "It looks that way."

"I'd like to meet him, and I'm sure he'd like to meet me."

The major cocked an eyebrow. "And why would he want to meet you?"

"Because I just saved his life, and I'm looking for a job."

"Just what kind of job are you looking for?"

"One that lets me kill as many Ukrainians as possible."

Sherrie held her position as events unfolded. She had her weapon trained on the Valkyrie patrol should things go south. Gunfire rattled from the Ukrainian side exactly on schedule, prompting the Valkyrie patrol to redirect their attention down the road as opposed to the staged scene. The less attention they paid to what was right in front of their eyes, the better.

She breathed a sigh of relief when Jack handed over his weapons voluntarily and climbed in the back of one of the vehicles before all three pulled away, leaving the massacre site behind. The bodies would be recovered by the approaching Ukrainian forces and given the proper burial they so richly deserved, for right now, it appeared their postmortem sacrifice had apparently succeeded.

Unfortunately, there was no way to know for sure. There were no tracking devices, no drones, only satellites to follow her friend and colleague. He had no way to communicate with them as they couldn't risk anything being found in a search. It would mean immediate death, or worse, death after torture.

He was on his own, with no extraction possible.

She activated her comms. "Control, Skylark. Come in, over."

Leroux responded. "This is Control Actual, go ahead, Skylark."

"Jackrabbit has been picked up by Valkyrie forces. It appears he left on friendly terms."

"You think they bought it?"

"I can't say for certain, but they didn't shoot him, so that's a good sign."

Leroux chuckled. "Always. Your status?"

"I'm going to make my way east. Keep an eye on him and give me a final destination. With his watch malfunctioning, I want to be nearby in case something goes wrong."

"Copy that, Skylark. Stay safe."

"I always do."

"Remember who you're talking to."

She grinned. "All right, all right. I always *try* to."

Valkyrie Encampment, Russian-Held Territory

East of Bakhmut, Ukraine

Jack stood outside what he assumed was the headquarters of the Valkyrie encampment, about five miles from the front lines. Heavy constant fighting could be heard to the west, but here things appeared relatively relaxed. The notorious mercenary group was made up mostly of ex-Russian Special Forces, Spetsnaz. It had been supplemented in recent months by inmates from Russian prisons, mostly used as cannon fodder, waves of the poor bastards thrown at the Ukrainian positions in the hopes that one or two would get through and do some damage.

A door opened and he was beckoned in. "The general will see you now."

Jack stepped through, his expert eye taking in everything. There was communications gear on a table nearby, several maps that were covered over, most likely for his benefit, and the man himself stood in the center of the room, his hands clasped behind his back, his presence dominating the space. This man was a force to be reckoned with, which was rather remarkable considering his history. He was a criminal long before he had become involved with Valkyrie, a man who had served time in prison, then afterward, opened a hot dog stand, parlaying that into a catering business that cooked for the Kremlin and the Russian president himself.

Through that association, they had become friends, and he had managed to take over Valkyrie with the Russian president's blessing. The mercenary group was used to doing the dirty work of the Russian Army in places like Syria and Libya, and various other hostile zones around the world.

And it was all controlled by this one man.

Konstantin Pikalov.

Or General Pikalov, as he had taken to calling himself.

"It looks like I owe you a debt of gratitude." He jerked his chin at a man standing to his right, his face covered by a balaclava with a painted jawbone that would no doubt scare trick-or-treaters. It was the man's eyes that were more intimidating. He held out a hand, gripping the photo that Jack had planted on one of the Ukrainian corpses. Jack noted the skull ring on the man's hand. "It looks like the Ukrainians were coming for me."

"It looks that way."

"What were you doing out there?"

"Minding my own business until they didn't mind theirs."

Pikalov chuckled. "So, I hear you wanted to meet me. What for?"

"I want to serve."

"Then join the army."

Jack grunted. "The army is not for me. They've got rules. I don't like rules."

"We have rules too."

"Your rules still allow you to get things done. I want to get things done."

Pikalov pursed his lips. "I like how you think. What did you have in mind?"

Jack indicated the photo. "It would appear your personal guard could be beefed up somewhat."

Pikalov laughed and turned to the man with the face covering. "Have Chekalov check him out. If he's clean, then put him on the detail. We can always use good men that aren't just meat sacks."

Jack smirked. "I won't be clean. I'll be as filthy as hell. Which is exactly what you want covering your ass."

Pikalov smiled. "I think I'm gonna like you."

Valkyrie Encampment, Russian-Held Territory

East of Bakhmut, Ukraine

Colonel Anton Chekalov climbed into the back of one of their mobile command centers. The quarters were cramped, but it was chockfull of state-of-the-art comms gear and could pull out on a moment's notice should it become necessary. He preferred the tents, but the tents didn't have the computer connections that were needed. "Did you get that FSB report yet?"

"Just printing it now, sir." One of the men reached over and grabbed a sheaf of paper off the printer and handed it over. "You're not gonna believe it. That's probably the craziest FSB report I've ever read."

Chekalov quickly scanned it. "This is one absolutely filthy bastard."

"He's perfect."

"Too perfect. Nobody is this bad and still alive." He reread the file. The number of engagements this guy had been involved with was impressive, but what he had reportedly done was disturbing even to him. Yet there were major gaps, which was rare. Their contacts at the FSB usually provided complete files, which meant, for some reason, even they were in the dark.

He had to dig deeper. Pikalov was taken with the man, and that could be dangerous. They were at too critical a point to put things at risk by bringing a stranger into the mix, no matter how impressive a file they might have.

The next few days could change the course of history.

And no new arrival could be allowed to put that at risk.

Operations Center 3, CIA Headquarters

Langley, Virginia

Leroux entered the state-of-the-art operations center buried in the bowels of CIA headquarters and waved at his team already in place. "Good morning, everyone." A round of greetings was the response as he took up his position in the center of the room. "Sorry I'm late. I had to meet with the Chief. What's the status?"

His second-in-command, Senior Analyst Sonya Tong, turned in her chair to face him. "They're starting a deep dive on his cover. We're getting calls and emails being sent to the units and prisons we've placed him in."

Leroux sat, logging into his station. "Let's hope this works. This is one of the deepest covers we've ever created. It's taken years. Now it's time to see if we did our jobs right or if we just handed Jack a death sentence."

"How will we know?" asked Randy Child, the team's tech wunderkind and youngest member.

Danny Packman, one of the senior analysts, gave him a look. "Well, if they kill him, that might be our first clue."

Child flipped him the bird. "You know what I mean. How long will they keep digging until they're satisfied?"

Leroux faced him. "Impossible to say. As long as nothing contradicts what they're checking out, he should be good. If he's alive at the end of the day, then I'd say it'll probably be fine. But with these people, you never know. Their leadership is psychotic, and they don't follow any rules. All we can do is pray the people who created this cover did their job right, or Jack is screwed."

Valkyrie Encampment, Russian-Held Territory

East of Bakhmut, Ukraine

Jack stood at ease, his hands clasped behind his back. The fact he had been welcomed once again into the headquarters building told him the boys and girls at Langley had done their jobs well. He just wished his state-of-the-art watch, disguised as a cheap Timex, worked so he could thank them. It had stopped working during his insertion into Ukraine, cutting him completely off from Langley now that he had infiltrated Valkyrie without comms.

"He checks out," said Colonel Chekalov, a man Jack recognized from the files he had memorized. This was a brutal man, responsible for several massacres in Syria, and God knows how many while a member of Spetsnaz. He wasn't to be underestimated. "There's a good chunk of his file that we couldn't get from the FSB, but I made a few calls. Turns out our friend here was part of Directorate Z."

General Pikalov cocked an eyebrow at the revelation Jack had been part of a Spetsnaz unit so top secret, the name was only whispered, and no one knew what they did. "Directorate Z. Interesting. So then, you've had quite a bit of experience."

Jack shrugged. "You could say that."

"Why did you leave?"

"Let's just say, when things go wrong, they always look for a scapegoat."

Chekalov eyed him. "And is that why you served five years in Black Dolphin Prison, for disobeying orders and slaughtering most of a village in Syria?"

Jack shrugged. "I had intel that an ISIS leader was hiding there. I led my unit in, the locals refused to identify him, Command said he was definitely there, so I made a decision. If the village wouldn't identify who he was, then there was only one way to make sure we got him."

Pikalov cocked an eyebrow. "You killed them all?"

"They were the enemy. I did what had to be done. Apparently, Command didn't agree with my decision. They were afraid if the press got ahold of it, the Motherland would look bad, so I was dishonorably discharged and thrown in prison."

"But it was your decision to kill everyone, including the civilians?"

"Yes. Our standing orders were to kill any collaborators. I did my duty and we were able to later identify the ISIS leader. They knew who they were protecting. I'd do the same thing again."

Pikalov regarded him for a moment. "Good. I don't like men who second-guess their decisions. You had your orders. You had a problem. You solved it. You succeeded in your mission. That's the exact type of soldier I want serving me. If there's an objective to take and there are civilians in the way, eliminate the civilians. They're all the enemy."

Chekalov shook the sheaf of papers he was holding. "You left prison a year ago. There's no record here of what you've been doing since."

"I've been killing Ukrainians."

Pikalov cocked an eyebrow. "Any reason why?"

Jack shrugged. "They're our enemy. And I didn't need a passport to get here."

"Who have you been fighting with?"

"No one. Just myself."

Chekalov's eyebrows shot up. "Wait a minute. Are you the Red Wolf we've been hearing about?"

Jack shrugged. "I prefer Jack."

"Jack?"

"As part of Directorate Z, I was trained to infiltrate NATO facilities as an American. I've gotten used to it, and prefer not to use my real name. There are people out there who aren't happy I'm out."

Pikalov scratched his chin, staring at him. "Jack. I like it. That'll really mess with their heads when they start seeing that show up in their reports." He extended a hand and Jack took it. "Welcome aboard, Jack."

Forward Operating Base Echo 62

Ukrainian-Controlled Territory, Ukraine

She stank. In fact, everyone at the Forward Operating Base did. There were no showers here, and even if there were, there was no time to use them. Soldiers were constantly rotating in and out of the front lines as the counter-offensive against the Russian invaders raged on.

While avoiding a Russian patrol, Sherrie's comms had failed and she had decided it was best to fall back to the Ukrainian FOB. This was her first opportunity to reach out to Langley. She couldn't talk with others around—nobody could know what was actually going on. Only the Ukrainian commander knew what had really happened earlier in the day.

She activated her Ukrainian-supplied comms. "Control, Skylark. Do you read, over?"

"This is Control Actual. Go ahead, Skylark."

She smiled at the relief in her boyfriend's voice, picturing him standing behind his station in the operations center. "I've extracted to the Ukrainian FOB after a comms failure. I'm secure. What's the status on Jackrabbit?"

"We've got him on satellite. He appears fine. They've given him his weapons back, so they seem to trust him."

"Has he established any way to communicate with us?"

"Negative. For now, the only way he can communicate is visually, which he won't risk unless it's something urgent. The Chief wants you to stay in theater in case we need to extract him."

"Of course. But I'll need some backup if that becomes necessary."

"Delta's on standby in Poland, but hopefully it won't come to that."

Somebody said something in the background.

"Standby." She tensed and Leroux cursed. "Take cover! Russian missiles are inbound on your location!"

Sherrie sprinted from the tent and shouted at the top of her lungs. "Russian missiles inbound!"

Everyone froze for a moment then there were shouts as her English warning was translated into Ukrainian. A siren sounded, sending everyone scrambling. Somebody grabbed her by the arm and she didn't resist, instead following the man, allowing herself to be herded down a set of wooden steps and into a bomb shelter. She rushed deep into the underground shelter then took a knee, covering her head. Somebody tossed her a helmet and she shoved it in place, fastening the strap just as the first missile hit, shaking the entire area. Dust and dirt fell from overhead and the lights flickered out. Her comms cut off as the front entrance collapsed, eliminating the last sliver of light.

Operations Center 3, CIA Headquarters

Langley, Virginia

Leroux stood, his mouth agape at the satellite image showing a devastated forward operating base, two Russian missiles having detonated only moments ago, clouds of dust and debris still billowing into the air preventing any view of the carnage. His stomach churned and he sucked in a deep breath.

Get control.

He pointed at Tong. "Notify Ukrainian Central Command of the airstrike and the need for search and rescue teams." His voice cracked as he turned to Danny Packman. "Keep trying to raise her."

"You got it, boss."

Tong turned to him. "Go take a few minutes. We've got this."

Leroux nodded, saying nothing, and left the room, his entire body trembling as he thought of the only woman he had ever loved, dead in a twisted mess, buried under the rubble of a Russian attack.

God, please don't let this be the end.

Forward Operating Base Echo 62

Ukrainian-Controlled Territory, Ukraine

Sherrie continued to cover her head, crouching on the floor, her back to the ceiling as everything around her collapsed. Something pinged off her helmet, ringing her bell for a moment, and she collapsed to the floor, struggling to regain her senses. Men and women around her were moaning and groaning, words exchanged in Ukrainian among the survivors of the Russian missile attack.

Someone nearby whimpered in pain, and as she regained her senses, she reached out, grasping in the darkness for the source. Her hand touched something and a man gasped.

"Are you all right?" she asked.

"I think I broke my leg," replied the man in heavily accented English.

During her efforts to locate him, she hadn't noticed that the bombing had stopped, that the collapse of their shelter had, at least for the moment, settled. Someone called out in Ukrainian, the tone suggesting a question was being asked, probably if everyone was all right. Voices sounded in the darkness, then a flashlight flickered on, then another, the beams slicing through the dust.

"I've got a wounded man here!" she announced.

Somebody scurried toward her and she moved aside, a medic taking over. She took the opportunity for a self-assessment, moving all her limbs and joints then feeling all over her body for any tender areas. She was a little bruised up, but as far as she could tell in the near pitch dark, she wasn't wounded, and where it hurt didn't suggest internal injuries.

She had gotten lucky.

More lights were on now, her companions mostly on their feet, tending to those not so lucky. The entrance had collapsed, or more accurately, the access to the entrance, likely buried by debris from one of the impacts. A beam at the center of the shelter had fallen, the thick piece of wood having snapped in the center allowing the ground overhead to fall in atop them, this structural failure the cause of most of the injuries.

A senior officer inside the shelter made the rounds, checking on everyone, and he stopped in front of her. "Are you all right?"

"Yes, sir. A little bruised up, but I'm good to go."

"That's good. Just sit tight. They'll have us dug out soon enough."

He moved on and she reactivated her comms tucked deep in her ear canal, but heard nothing but static. She made her way toward the collapsed entrance and tried once again. "Control, this is Skylark. Do you read, over?"

There was a squelching sound, a voice heavily broken up replying, but she couldn't make out any of the words, though the fact they had heard her attempt should be enough to let them know she was alive.

Shouts from outside had someone slapping her on the back. "Step back, miss. They're starting to clear the entrance. We wouldn't want anything to fall on you."

She reluctantly followed the order, and within minutes, a sliver of light from outside had broken through, cheers from her companions releasing some of the tension they all felt at their predicament. She turned her attention to helping with the wounded, her first aid training extensive, though much of what was taught at the Farm centered around how to treat yourself, since operatives typically flew solo.

She helped bandage up a head wound as the efforts to clear the entrance continued. After about ten minutes, enough of the debris was moved away for a signal to finally get through.

"Skylark, Control, come in, over."

It was Tong's voice, which surprised her.

"Control, Skylark, I read you, over."

"Thank God, we were beginning to think the worst. What's your status?"

"I'm a little bruised up, but nothing broken, nothing bleeding. My hosts are clearing the entrance to the bomb shelter now. Hopefully we'll be out shortly. Tell Control Actual not to worry, Skylark still flies."

"Acknowledged, Skylark. I'll let him know right away. Is there anything you need from us?"

Sherrie finished with the dressing, smiling at the young man and patting him on the cheek. "A day at the spa?"

Tong chuckled. "That's a tall order on the front line, Skylark, but I'll see what I can do."

"You do that, Control. Skylark, out."

Somebody tapped her on the shoulder. "Time to leave."

She twisted around to see the entrance open. "Wounded first."

The senior officer shook his head. "No, VIP American first. I know why you're here, and your mission is far more important than ours."

She wagged a finger at him. "You're not supposed to know that."

He smirked. "If a commanding officer can't trust his second-in-command with what's going on, then my country's in bigger trouble than it already is."

She smiled. "Fine, he's forgiven, but don't tell anyone else. I'd hate to have to kill you all."

Bakhmut, Ukraine

Jack's face remained neutral, but inside his heart was breaking. It was utter devastation on a scale he had never thought he would see outside of archival footage of the Second World War. Bakhmut was destroyed. There was nothing left to fight for, yet they continued, both sides desperate for the win, the battle no longer for a city, but for bragging rights that they had beat their opponent.

It was ridiculous.

It was something the world thought it had outgrown, that Europe had thought was relegated to the distant past, yet here it was, in the present, as vicious and violent as it ever had been, the weapons more sophisticated in some cases, but the brutality the same. Man killing man, and for what reason? Because a psychotic dictator who clung to the past, a past that wasn't even real, today's memories of the Soviet Union a nostalgic fallacy.

This had to stop, but how?

The Russians appeared determined to continue to fight despite losing, and perhaps that was all the proof needed that Leroux's theory, that the Russian transfer of nukes was in preparation for a final solution to the problem, might just be accurate. Could the carnage of Hiroshima, of Nagasaki, be repeated on an even greater scale in the coming days? Could Kyiv be flattened, its millions of citizens vaporized by a madman hell-bent on restoring Russian honor and dignity that had never existed?

Gunfire erupted to his left and he turned his back toward it, grabbing Pikalov and hauling him closer. Jack grunted twice as he took two rounds to the back, the other members of the security detail opening fire, announcing the all-clear a moment later, the lone enemy's weapon silenced.

Jack let go of Pikalov then rotated his shoulders as Chekalov stepped over and examined his flak jacket. He pulled out the two rounds and showed them to Jack and the general. "You're gonna be tender for a few days."

Jack grunted. "Wouldn't be the first time some coward shot me in the back."

Pikalov slapped him on the arm. "It looks like I owe you my life once again."

"Just doing my job."

"And doing it well. From now on, you're by my side. I think you might just be my good luck charm."

CIA Headquarters
Langley, Virginia

There was a knock on the outer door to the bathroom and Leroux looked up, struggling to control his emotions and failing miserably. At the moment, he was alone. The hinges creaked and he held his breath.

"Chris, are you in here?"

He exhaled. It was Tong. "Yeah."

"I just talked to Sherrie. She's all right."

He cried out in relief and stood, opening the door to the stall he had taken refuge in, and rushed around the corner to see Tong with an arm extended, holding the door open. Her smile was quickly replaced with concern at the sight of his tear-stained cheeks.

"Oh, you poor dear." She stepped inside and took him in her arms. She squeezed him tight and he held her, racked with sobs at the fantasies his mind had imagined for the woman he loved, and relief that she was all right. "I spoke to her. Nothing broken, just a few bumps and bruises.

She said to tell you…" It was Tong's turn for her voice to crack. "Skylark still flies," she whispered.

Leroux sniffed hard, releasing his grip on the woman he knew loved him, and for whom he had feelings as well, feelings he of course would never act upon.

She forced a smile, staring up into his eyes. "Are you going to be all right?"

He sniffed. "Yes, now that I know she's okay." He wiped a thumb across her cheek, removing a stray tear. "Are you going to be all right?"

She inhaled deeply and stepped back. "Of course, why wouldn't I?"

It was just a cover, and he decided not to make her more uncomfortable by pressing the issue. "Good. Get back to your post. I'm going to wash up here. I'll be there in a minute."

"All right."

The door swung open and Child pulled up, startled to see them both in the men's room. "Oh, hey guys. I was looking for you. I just thought you should both know that Jack has moved closer to the front line."

Leroux wiped his cheeks clear with his fingers. "How close?"

"Oh, I don't know. Within twenty feet of it?"

Valkyrie Encampment, Russian-Held Territory

East of Bakhmut, Ukraine

Jack finished his business, wiping his ass with Russian toilet paper that had to be 60 grit. It was the small comforts that you missed when out in the field, and good toilet paper was one of them. American toilet paper—two-ply minimum, three-ply preferred. Was there a four-ply? There had to be. If you could order a Wendy's Baconator with extra bacon, America had to have invented four if not eight-ply TP. He would check when he got home.

With Pikalov now trusting him after today's earlier events, he had free reign of the compound and had taken advantage, using various excuses to explore the entire facility. Thousands of troops were stationed here, heading in and out nonstop as they were rotated to the front lines and back. There were half a dozen large wooden buildings at the rear of the compound that in all the time he had been here, he hadn't seen anyone enter. That had him curious since space was at a premium.

He walked with purpose toward one of them, casually glancing around to make sure no one saw him, then tried the door. It was locked but flimsy. He put a shoulder into it and the lock splintered. He shoved the door open and stepped inside, listening for a moment. He heard nothing inside or out that indicated he had been detected. He closed the door behind him. Light poured in from windows overhead, mounted high on the walls, revealing what could only be described as a warehouse stacked to the rafters with crates.

He stepped over to the nearest pallet and popped one of the lids, finding 7.62-millimeter ammo. He checked the labels on the crates, the entire pallet filled with ammo that fit the AK-47 that seemed to be the preferred assault rifle here. More pallets were stacked from front to back, the warehouse loaded with ammo, grenades, mortar shells, and more.

Valkyrie's leader had been complaining publicly for weeks now that the Russian military wasn't supplying him with what he needed to win the battle in Bakhmut, but what was in this warehouse alone proved that was a complete and utter lie. There was enough ammo to provision an army for weeks of intense battle, and this was just one building. He had to think the rest were filled with the same.

"What the hell are you doing here?"

Jack casually turned toward the voice to find a colonel stepping through the broken door, followed by three others. "Demonstrating how pathetic security is around here. Do you realize that if I were a Ukrainian operative or, hell, Russian FSB, our secret would be out?"

The man eyed him. "What secret?"

"Don't play stupid. We're going on social media telling the world that we're running out of ammo and blaming the Russian military for shorting us on our supplies, yet we've got millions of rounds here. All it would take is for one of our enemies to infiltrate, take some photos, and the lie is public. What will the general do then?"

The colonel appeared confused. "I...don't know."

Jack pressed. "Do you think he'll be able to proceed with his plan?"

"I guess not." The man's eyes narrowed. "Wait, show me your hands."

"What?"

Guns aimed at him.

"Show me your hands."

Jack raised both.

The colonel sneered, holding up a fist with one of the prized rings. "Unless you have one of these, you shouldn't know anything about the plan. I think we found our infiltrator."

US V Corps Headquarters (Forward)

Camp Kościuszko, Poland

"You mean to tell me that artificial intelligence doesn't scare the shit out of you?"

Sergeant Leon "Atlas" James shrugged at his best friend's question. "The military applications, absolutely, but outside of that, no."

Sergeant Carl "Niner" Sung stared at his impossibly muscled friend in disbelief at his lack of concern. "What about all the people who are going to lose their jobs?"

"You're looking at it the wrong way."

"What do you mean?"

"You're ignoring the opportunity here. Remember, when they invented the car and it took over as the main mode of transportation, everybody in the horse trade pretty much lost their jobs., but they didn't just sit at home and cry about it. They retrained. They got other jobs. The people who lose their jobs to AI over the coming years will retrain and get other jobs."

Sergeant Will "Spock" Lightman cocked an eyebrow. "Yeah, but I think what a lot of people are worried about is that there won't be any jobs. When the horse and buggy was replaced by the car, there was still the car. It was built by humans, maintained by humans, operated by humans. But with AI, I think the worry is that you're not replacing one technology with another. You're replacing the human technology. So, the next evolution of that job involves far fewer people. You're going to require programmers and what not, but if you take an entire call center, let's say a thousand people providing front-line support, and replace it with an AI that does the job better and more accurately and far cheaper, those thousand employees are gone, out of work. And it's not like they can retrain to be people who develop AI applications, because out of those thousand, maybe you need ten or twenty. So, while replacing the horse and buggy with the car meant millions of jobs were lost, there were millions of jobs created at the same time. With AI, that doesn't happen."

Command Sergeant Major Burt "Big Dog" Dawson, who had stayed out of the conversation so far, busy reading the latest updates from the Pentagon and Langley on the situation they might be about to get themselves in, finally chimed in. "I think that's the point, though, isn't it?"

As the commander of Bravo Team, a unit of the elite 1st Special Forces Operational Detachment–Delta, commonly known to the public as the Delta Force, his men all faced him, curious for his take. "I was watching a report a couple of weeks ago that was quite interesting. There was the idea that AI could replace most jobs. At the moment, that sounds ridiculous, but you have to remember what the limitation on robots is right now. It's that they can't think for themselves. They have to be programmed for every situation. But if the AI advances enough to where it doesn't need to be programmed for every situation, that it could figure out how to deal with something unexpected, just like the human brain does, then you can put that intelligence into machines that perform manual tasks like plumbers, electricians, roofers, everything. So, in theory, most jobs could be done either by an AI system, or an AI-enabled machine."

Niner stared at him. "That sounds like a horror show. Terminator level shit. Hell, Matrix level."

Atlas grunted. "I think you mean the other way around. Terminator's gotta be worse than the Matrix."

"I think they would both suck."

"At least in the Matrix, though, you're alive. Terminator, they're out trying to kill you."

"Yeah, well, maybe you might enjoy having a lightbulb stuck up your ass. I think I'd rather be fighting on my feet or dead."

Sergeant Gerry "Jimmy Olsen" Hudson raised a finger. "Um, I don't think they had a light bulb up their asses. I think they were the light bulbs."

Spock gave him a look. "I think we're straying from the point." He held out a hand. "Please, BD, continue."

Dawson chuckled. "I don't think the question is what do we do when there are no jobs left, because that's quite a ways off. But what do you do when, let's say, half the population ten years from now is unemployed, because the robots have replaced them?"

Niner shrugged. "Tax the shit out of those who have jobs, so we can pay for people to sit at home?"

"Unfortunately, that's how some people probably would try to deal with the situation. But think about it. What's the motivation for a company to replace an employee with a computer system?"

Atlas shrugged. "It's cheaper?"

"Exactly. So, if you've replaced the bulk of your workforce, or even just a healthy percentage, with far cheaper artificial intelligence-driven equipment and machines, doesn't that mean whatever service or product you're offering becomes cheaper to make?"

Heads bobbed.

"Exactly. So, think about it. Let's say it costs half a million dollars to build a home. But because you've replaced the labor involved to be 90% machine-driven, and keep in mind, all the products that go into the home, lumber, drywall, whatever, is cheaper as well, because at the manufacturing end, it's now all robots, that half million dollars to build, and by extension, the mortgage you need, is far lower. And that's true with everything in your life. Your car is cheaper. Your house is cheaper. Your groceries are cheaper. Everything you need to live is cheaper because you've taken the human element out of the manufacturing and operating expenses. So, now if you needed $100,000 a year to live today, but suddenly everything was half as expensive, do you still need $100,000? Maybe you only need $75,000. Maybe you only need $50,000. And if you only need $50,000, then why are you working forty hours a week? Maybe you only need to work twenty to enjoy the same lifestyle, which frees up a job for someone else."

Niner stared at him for a moment. "So, what you're saying is, AI makes things cheaper, which brings the cost of living down, which reduces how much someone needs to earn, which frees up the jobs that remain to be shared."

"Exactly."

Atlas grunted. "I'm not so sure that utopian vision would work. People are greedy. They'll want to keep working the forty hours so that they can have an even better lifestyle."

"Oh, there'd definitely be a lot of people who did that, especially at the beginning, but eventually more and more people will decide that they would rather have more leisure time than money in the bank."

Spock grinned. "So, what we're saying is we're heading toward a Star Trek-type world."

Dawson shrugged. "Doesn't sound too bad."

Niner shook his head. "The only thing Star Trek about all this is that right now we're developing the precursor to the Borg."

"True, definite possibility, but unfortunately the genie's out of the bottle now. We have to keep pushing forward because you know damn well our enemies are."

Atlas jabbed a meaty finger at Dawson. "Now, *that's* the truth."

Jimmy sighed. "All this intellectual talk is hurting my head, though I vote when we get back home we have a Terminator marathon at the Unit. One weekend, all six movies."

Niner's eyes narrowed. "Six?"

"Terminator Salvation."

Niner batted a hand. "I don't count that one. Arnie wasn't in it."

Atlas eyed him. "Sure he was."

"No, he wasn't."

"Yes, he was. Near the end of the movie, they did that scene with him all muscled up like he was in the early eighties."

Niner's jaw slowly dropped. "Oh, yeah, I forgot about that. Eh, it's not really Arnie, is it? It's just computer-generated." He pointed a finger at the others. "And that's part of the problem too, isn't it? How long is it gonna be before we go to a movie and nobody's actually in it? I read something just a few weeks ago where they were saying that AI might be used to generate all the extras in a movie. How long before the main actors are replaced with CGI and Brad Pitt is just licensing his likeness, but not actually acting?"

"It's already possible to do," said Jimmy. "It would be cool, though, to see new movies with some of the greats from the past that are either dead or too old to do the action roles they used to."

Spock agreed. "That would be cool, though my man Harrison Ford did a damn good job pretending he was a hell of a lot younger in the new Indiana Jones movie."

"True, but he's an enigma."

Atlas raised his arms, flexing his massive biceps. "Forget that." He kissed the left then the right. "If AI can be used for anything, I want to put myself in my favorite movies."

Niner's eyes widened. "Oh, my God, that'd be so awesome!"

"Me in your favorite movies? I agree."

Niner wrapped his arms around Atlas. "I can picture it now. You on your horse. Me on mine. Brokeback Mountain with a brother and a Korean."

Atlas groaned as the rest of them burst out in laughter. He shoved his friend aside. "You and Angela have to have a serious conversation."

"Invite Vanessa and she might be okay with it."

Spock cocked an eyebrow. "I think this just went from Brokeback Mountain to Caligula."

Jimmy raised a hand. "Count me in."

"To which one?"

"Caligula, of course." Jimmy sighed. "Ah, yes, Roman orgies and vomitoriums. Whatever happened to the good old days?"

Niner leaned forward. "I thought I read somewhere that that vomitorium thing was actually bullshit."

Jimmy shrugged. "I'm not a historian. Next time we see Professor Acton, I'll be sure to ask."

Niner gestured at the tablet Dawson had been reading the briefing notes on. "Speaking of the Doc, does he have anything to do with this op we're on standby for?"

"Not this time. We've got two CIA operatives that are currently in Ukraine that might need extraction."

"Who?"

"Right now, Jack has infiltrated Valkyrie."

"Jack who?" asked Atlas.

"Just Jack."

"Oh, that Jack. Who's the other one?"

"Sherrie White."

Jimmy whistled. "Now, *she's* a hottie."

Dawson gave him a look. "And I have no doubt she'd be delighted to hear you say that."

Jimmy held up his hands. "Sorry. I don't think I'm ever gonna get used to a society where everybody's offended by everything, and the double standard reigns."

Spock cocked an eyebrow. "Double standard?"

"I'm sorry, but I've overheard enough conversations from tables of women or even, hell, at home when the other halves don't think I can hear them, and they're talking about guys and their smiles, their asses, their penis lengths—"

Niner's eyes bugged out. "Penis lengths? They talk about that shit?"

Atlas elbowed him. "Don't worry, little man. Size doesn't matter."

"Easy to say for the human tripod."

Spock snickered then brought them back on track. "If we're going in for an extraction, does that mean we're going up against Valkyrie?"

"It could," replied Dawson.

Atlas smiled. "Good. I wouldn't mind taking out a few of those bastards."

Dawson agreed. "Me too. Unfortunately, there are over ten thousand of those bastards where we'd be heading, so the odds aren't exactly in our favor."

Outside the Valkyrie Encampment, Russian-Held Territory

East of Bakhmut, Ukraine

Sherrie inched forward in her ghillie suit, none the worse for wear after her ordeal in the bomb shelter. A Ukrainian Special Forces team had helped her insert past the front lines only a short time ago, and it hadn't taken her long to reach the Valkyrie camp. The perimeter was reasonably well-defended. A heavy chain-link fence topped with barbed wire surrounded the complex. Guard towers, positioned within sight of each other, were all manned, though the guards didn't seem to be paying too much attention. This was an undisciplined, or more likely overconfident, force.

She peered through her binoculars at the building Langley said Jack had just entered and cursed as four men followed moments later.

This can't be good.

She readied her crossbow. A gun wasn't an option here. A single shot would reveal her position and they would be down on her in no time—then she would be of no help to anybody. She aimed through the scope, making a note of the wind and the distance as she watched the proceedings through the open door. The conversation appeared civil.

Then it took a turn.

Jack darted forward as she loosed a bolt.

Valkyrie Encampment, Russian-Held Territory

East of Bakhmut, Ukraine

Jack crushed the colonel's windpipe with a fist to the throat, then drew his Makarov pistol, putting two rounds in each of the other three men before they could react. He put two more in the gasping colonel, silencing him. It was all over in seconds. He holstered his weapon and noticed that one of his targets had a crossbow bolt in the back. He peered through the door and grinned at whom he assumed was Sherrie somewhere beyond the fence line. He yanked the bolt free and whipped it behind the crates. He couldn't have anyone knowing she might be out there.

He grabbed a cellphone from the colonel's pocket and took photos of the ammo and the crates, sending them to a CIA number in Moscow, then tossed it on the ground beside the body as others came rushing in.

"What the hell happened here?" asked Chekalov, the shock in his voice clear.

Jack pointed at the phone. "I caught them taking photos of our supplies, and heard them talking about how they'd have a life on Easy Street if they let Moscow know that we were lying about our ammo shortage."

Pikalov stepped inside, frowning, apparently having overheard Jack's report as he approached. He stared down at the body of the colonel. "I can't believe he would betray me. He's been with me for years."

Jack shrugged. "Everyone has a price."

Pikalov eyed him. "Do you?"

"Not one that anyone can meet."

Pikalov laughed. "I like you. Join me for dinner, we have much to discuss."

"I could eat." Jack jerked a thumb at the crates. "And then will you tell me why we have enough ammo to start a second front?"

Another laugh and Pikalov held up his fist, revealing one of the skull rings. "Not until you earn one of these."

Jack eyed it. "And how do I do that?"

"Prove your loyalty, and that you're willing to do anything I ask of you."

Jack smirked. "Then I guess I'm already well on my way to getting one of those."

"You just might be."

Outside the Valkyrie Encampment, Russian-Held Territory

East of Bakhmut, Ukraine

Sherrie breathed a sigh of relief as Jack stepped out of the building and into the sunlight with Pikalov and the others, still armed. Whatever story he had told them they had evidently bought. During her training at the Farm, she had been taught that it didn't matter the size of the lie, it was the delivery. Confidence was key, and spies like Jack and Kane oozed confidence. She was still learning, but had already told some doozies while on assignment and was still here to talk about it.

A body was carried out on a stretcher, signaling to her the end of the episode, at least for now. She slowly crawled backward, away from the fence line. There was nothing else she could do here. Her intervention was likely a one-time thing. The best thing for her to do now was to get clear. If she were captured, they would know she was working with Jack. It was simply too much of a coincidence for him to show up, somehow foil an internal security threat, while she was nearby with a crossbow that had taken out one of those supposedly killed by him.

Her comms squawked in her ear and Tong's voice issued a warning. "Skylark, Control. A security sweep is starting. You need to get out of there now."

"Copy that," she whispered, turning around and pushing to her feet, rushing through the brush at a crouch as the sound of dogs and their handlers filled her ears. It was a standard patrol sent out early, probably due to what had just happened, but it didn't matter. If the dogs picked up her scent and she was still here, that would be the end. The barking intensified as did the shouts, Tong confirming what she already feared.

"The dogs have your scent. You've got to hurry."

She reached the river and stripped out of her ghillie suit, the approaching dogs getting louder. She rolled the suit into a ball and stuffed it into her backpack, then pressed a button on the pack, automatically inflating an air pouch. She waded out into the water then fell backward into it, arching her back as she spread her arms out, allowing the current to carry her away, her backpack bobbing beside her.

The water was cold, though not frigid, the midday sun warm. The barking in the distance faded as she steadied her breathing, adrenaline good in a tense situation, but just a taste of it— too much would give her the shakes. She kicked to the riverbank then pulled herself out, quickly finding new cover before assessing her situation.

That had been close.

Too close.

"Skylark, Control Actual. I don't think we can risk you going back in. They know someone was out there, they just don't know who or why."

Sherrie had to agree with Leroux. "Any indication they suspect Jack?"

"Negative. It looks like he's still with Pikalov. So far, it looks like he got away with it."

Valkyrie Encampment, Russian-Held Territory

East of Bakhmut, Ukraine

"What are your thoughts on the war?"

Jack sat across from Pikalov, a bottle of Stoli vodka on the table with two glasses. It appeared they were to have a private dinner. No one else. It was obviously a test to feel him out to see if he shared their values. It was his chance to perhaps be welcomed into the inner circle, and if he played his cards right, he just might glean some sense of what was going on, since men like Pikalov had egos so big they couldn't help but boast.

"I think the war is going piss poorly."

"And why do you think that?"

"A lack of resolve from the leadership in Moscow."

Pikalov cocked an eyebrow. "The president?"

Jack was careful, well aware of how close Pikalov and the president were. "No, the president's orders were clear. It was the military leadership who failed in their execution. To have the entire opening salvos of the war dependent upon a single airplane with a single Spetsnaz unit was stupid. The Americans warned the Ukrainians and they blew it out of the sky before it had a chance to land and take over the airport. There was an intelligence failure, but there was also a lack of planning. If we had taken that airport on the first night, we could have flown in thousands of troops over the coming days, taken Kyiv, and the war would have been over. With their leadership sacked, there'd be no coordination among their military units, and our forces would have simply rolled across their territory right to the Polish border. It would have been over in a couple of weeks. But instead, we had arrogant planning, the airport wasn't taken, and Kyiv remained intact, giving them time to mount a defense."

Pikalov's head slowly bobbed. "An interesting assessment, one of which I happen to agree with. If Moscow had allowed my men to take the airport, it would have been done."

"Of that, I have no doubt."

"So, how do you think we can win this war?"

"Less pussyfooting around. Most of the world under the thumb of the Americans already hate us and have enacted sanctions against us. So, what else do we have to lose? We should be hitting Ukrainian infrastructure hard. Take out their power plants, take out their water treatment plants, take out their railroads, their highways, their airports. Who cares how many civilians die as long as we win in the end?"

"So, civilian casualties don't concern you?"

Jack shrugged. "If we could win without killing a single civilian, that'd be great. But that's not the real world. In World War Two, did we concern ourselves with such nonsense? We bombed the shit out of German cities, leveled them, killed millions, and we won. If we had concerned ourselves with trying to separate innocent Germans from the Nazis, we'd probably all be speaking German right now."

"Heaven forbid! Can you imagine?"

Jack chuckled, taking a shot of vodka. "Too guttural, almost as bad as Arabic."

Pikalov spat. "If there's one language I hate, it's that one. It's all yelling and anger even when they're reading love poetry."

Jack smirked. "I'll take your word for it, since I'm not an expert in Arabic romantic literature."

Pikalov roared with laughter, downing his glass, and Jack refilled them both. Pikalov leaned back and folded his arms. "So, what you're saying is we need to get tougher, to not concern ourselves about public opinion, and simply do whatever's necessary to win."

Jack waved a hand. "I'm no general, I'm just a soldier. But in my inexpert opinion, yes. Throughout history, the military has never concerned itself with civilian casualties. That's a modern concept. If you take the horror out of war, then people forget why we should avoid them."

"We should avoid war?"

"Every soldier wants peace, and I'm no different. However, again, this is the real world where peace isn't always an option, especially when our enemies keep lining up to tear us down. Sometimes you punch the bully in the nose, make him taste his own blood. Only then does he respect you."

Pikalov regarded him, scratching at his five o'clock shadow. "So, would you agree with our president that the greatest catastrophe of the twentieth century was the collapse of the Soviet Union?"

Jack flicked his wrist. "While I don't believe the Soviet Union was everything that some people think it was, there was no doubt that we were feared, we were respected, and we weren't messed with. It was before my time. I was barely out of diapers when it collapsed. But when I see the state of things today, I have to agree with the president that things would be much better if the Soviet Union had remained intact and simply adjusted to the times. Ukraine would still be ours, so we wouldn't be in this war, we wouldn't be giving our nuclear weapons to insignificant countries like Belarus, and NATO wouldn't have bases in the Baltics."

There was a knock at the door. "Come."

It opened and a group from the mess hall brought in their food, ending the conversation temporarily, which was unfortunate. He was hoping to get some inkling as to what Pikalov thought of the nuke transfer.

They were left alone once again and Pikalov picked up his utensils. "I hate to talk politics while I eat." He stabbed his steak. "Seen any good movies lately?"

Operations Center 3, CIA Headquarters

Langley, Virginia

Morrison stood beside Leroux in the middle of the operations center, the photos Jack had taken of the Valkyrie warehouse shown on the main display.

"Any estimates?"

"Several hundred thousand rounds, plus thousands of grenades. That's just this one warehouse." Leroux pointed to a photo in the upper right corner, taken by satellite earlier. "We've got half a dozen identical buildings. They could be empty, they could be full. There's no way to know right now. Either way, this certainly shows that Pikalov's complaining on Telegram is all lies."

Tong faced them. "But to what end? They're fighting Ukrainians on the side of the Russians, they're funded and supplied by Moscow, and those weapons would help them win the battle. He's claiming he's losing hundreds if not thousands of men. He's blaming the military leadership, yet he's got all this weaponry sitting there. Why?"

Child spun in his chair, staring at the ceiling. "Maybe he plans on selling it on the black market."

Leroux and Morrison both turned toward the young man, who dropped his foot, killing his spin. Child suddenly appeared uncomfortable under their scrutiny.

"It was just an idea."

Morrison wagged a finger. "And it's a good one. Could that be it? Could it be simple greed? They keep asking Moscow for more and more ammo, Moscow sends it, they use some of it in the battle, just enough to keep the fight going. Remember, they're not sending their best troops in, the guys who've been loyal to the organization for years, they're sending in the cannon fodder, the prisoners they forced to join. They don't care if those guys die. They get extra ammo, they ship it off to their other interests in the Middle East and Africa. It saves them money. They don't have to buy it themselves. Or, like you said, they sell the supplies to other less-than-honest brokers. That stuff could end up in the hands of terrorists, Third-World regimes, or on the streets."

"It's as good a theory as any," agreed Leroux. "And right now, I can't think of any other reason why they'd be stockpiling ammo besides that. Hopefully, Jack will be able to figure things out." He jerked his chin toward a live satellite feed. "He's been alone with Pikalov for almost twenty minutes, and Pikalov knows that Jack is fully aware of the stockpile. It has to come up in their conversation."

Morrison pursed his lips as he stared at the photos once again. "Jack might bring it up, but I highly doubt that Pikalov will give him an explanation. There's no way he trusts him enough yet."

Valkyrie Encampment, Russian-Held Territory

East of Bakhmut, Ukraine

"I think the first one's the best. Classic Clint Eastwood, classic good old Hollywood violence."

Jack's head bobbed as he chewed one of the toughest steaks he had ever eaten. He swallowed then took a swig of wine to force it the rest of the way down. "Definitely. Dirty Harry was the best, but I enjoyed The Dead Pool as well. Magnum Force was pretty good, but I thought the others were weak."

Pikalov grunted. "Sudden Impact was painful, though it had the best line." He broke out into an Eastwood impression. "Go ahead, make my day."

Jack laughed at the not-too-bad imitation. "Pretty good, sir."

Pikalov toasted him with a raised glass. "I've been practicing."

Jack raised his own glass. "It shows."

Pikalov leaned back, pushing his plate away. "You can't really make movies like that anymore. Not in America. Kill hundreds of people on screen in horribly violent ways and audiences eat it up, but have a cop delivering justice to pieces of shit that deserve to die, and that's frowned upon."

"Yeah, I grew up after the fall and we got access to all that Western culture all at once. I remember my dad would come home every Friday after work with a bundle of videos and we would watch old Clint Eastwood movies, Charles Bronson, Lee Marvin, all the old greats. The violence was incredible, and I know it had my dad wondering what it was so many had been craving." Jack jerked his chin out the window toward the warehouse. "If you think about it, there's enough ammo in that building to fight a war, but America probably goes through more ammo on their own streets every month."

Pikalov grunted. "You're right. And our president agrees. He recognizes what's happening, not only within our borders, but with our neighbors. The violence is getting out of control and it's because there are too many apologists. The only thing that can save us from the corrupt West and its immoral values is a strong leader. Once we win this war, it's just the beginning. We'll reestablish—"

There was an urgent knock at the door and Pikalov frowned, clearly displeased with the interruption. "Come!"

The door opened and Chekalov entered. "Sorry to interrupt your dinner, sir, but our perimeter security patrol found something."

"What?"

"The dogs caught a scent just outside the fence line. They followed it to the river and found footprints, but no one was there. They tracked them back and they stopped at the tree line just outside the fence. Someone was definitely there."

Pikalov rose. "Any evidence they breached our perimeter?"

"None yet, but we're checking." He lowered his voice slightly, glancing at Jack. "We might need to advance our plans."

Jack regarded him. "And just what plans are those?"

Pikalov wagged a finger then tapped his ring. "You're not on the inside yet, but keep proving yourself and you will be." He gestured toward the door. "Now leave. I have to meet with my senior staff."

Jack rose. "Yes, sir."

"And Jack?"

"Yes, sir?"

"Go take a shower."

Jack grinned as he did a pit check before leaving the room, making note of the various men entering, all showing their ring to the guards, some with covered faces that had him wondering what their motivations were. Was it to hide their identity from satellites or drones? Did they want to remain anonymous for some reason? The real question was whether they revealed their faces once inside, or was the ring enough?

And what was about to be discussed?

It was a question that had to be answered.

Operations Center 3, CIA Headquarters

Langley, Virginia

Leroux sat, relieved now that Sherrie was secure, at least temporarily. She was far enough away from the base that the Valkyrie forces wouldn't bother searching for her, her decision to take the river a smart one. It killed the trail. And while the patrols continued to search around the perimeter, they hadn't expanded their search.

"There's Jack," said Tong, pointing.

He stared at the display. The live satellite feed zoomed in to show Jack leaving the building where he had been with Pikalov during all this. He walked casually away then, as he turned to head between two buildings, he tapped three times by his eye before disappearing.

Child squinted. "What does that mean?"

"He wants eyes on something."

"But what?"

Leroux pursed his lips. "It has to be the meeting. It looked like all the commanders went into that building as Jack was leaving." He pointed at Tong. "Get me Sherrie."

She tapped at her station, then gave him a thumbs-up as he fit his headset in place.

"Skylark, Control Actual. Come in, over."

"This is Skylark. Go ahead."

"Jack's called for eyes on a meeting. You're just within range. We need you to deploy a micro drone."

"Roger that. But how do we communicate what we saw to Jack?"

Leroux shook his head. "We'll figure that part out when we have something to tell him."

Valkyrie Encampment, Russian-Held Territory

East of Bakhmut, Ukraine

Jack stood under the hot water, allowing it to pour over his body, washing the lathered soap away. It had been days since he had properly bathed, and even longer since he had access to hot water. The Valkyrie guys had it easy compared to the regular troops. Diesel generators roared all over the camp, supplying power not only to lights, but to luxuries. They were clearly well-supplied despite the posts on social media.

Pikalov's tantrums and diatribes against the Russian military leadership were now legendary, and reported on regularly, with those who understood such things pointing out how he never directly criticized the Russian president who had given him his start. Pikalov had been a criminal, convicted of robbery and fraud and sentenced to twelve years at the age of twenty. He had served his time, then when he was a free man, decided to get into the food business, turning a food cart into a catering empire. That caught the eye of the Russian president, Pikalov becoming a trusted confidant over the years. He eventually became part of Valkyrie, then took it over, leading tens of thousands of the most brutal mercenaries in existence. The corporate empire he now managed was worth a fortune, with security operations in several Third-World countries, as well as mining and other business concerns.

But there was something more going on here that didn't make sense. These men had plenty of fuel, vast amounts of ammo, and remained a large contingent, despite their heavy casualties. Most of those lost in the battle for Bakhmut were cannon fodder, conscripts from the prisons sent out with little equipment or training in an attempt to overwhelm the Ukrainian positions with sheer numbers, and to draw down enemy ammo so they would be defenseless when the more experienced troops entered the fray.

And it was working. But at what cost? Why would a general send so many to their deaths and hold back their ammo, hold back their equipment that could save them? Was it to reinforce his lie? The more casualties on the battlefield that he could blame on a lack of supplies might mean Moscow would send even more. Or were the casualties a lie? Were they actually far fewer?

He turned off the water and toweled himself off. There was definitely something wrong here. And as long as he was on the outside, there was no way he would figure out what that was.

South of the Valkyrie Encampment, Russian-Held Territory
East of Bakhmut, Ukraine

The sun was low on the horizon and Sherrie didn't want to risk being picked up by a good set of eyes on the ball. She sat cross-legged in front of her laptop, a tarp covering her as she monitored the progress of the micro drone she had launched several minutes ago, the sophisticated device on autopilot, heading toward the precise GPS coordinates provided by Langley.

The device approached the target building, the computer analyzing the image and identifying the windows. She tapped the most likely candidate and the drone approached, revealing a group of men sitting at a table. She activated the listening mode and the drone attached to the glass, picking up the vibrations, allowing her and everyone back home to listen in.

And what was revealed had her skin crawling.

Operations Center 3, CIA Headquarters

Langley, Virginia

"We'll be going in tomorrow. We can't risk waiting. We'll take Rostov and set up our temporary HQ there. Once we're confident there'll be no resistance, we'll send the column to Moscow."

Leroux glanced over at the update, the computer identifying the voice as that of Pikalov, those who didn't speak Russian, like himself, listening to the live translation through their headsets.

"And if we encounter resistance?"

"We take them out. It's essential nothing stops us. That'll be your job, Bogatov. You have to reach the Ministry of Defense and arrest the leadership for their betrayal of Russia's military and its people. Their lack of success on the battlefield cannot be chalked up to mere incompetence. This is intentional, designed to make our nation appear weak, and by extension, our president. We've proven what a well-led army, independent of Moscow's leadership, can accomplish with a lack of supplies. We have been victorious where everyone else failed. And now, we will take out those who would lead our nation into an abyss that can only serve the West. We have been betrayed. Our nation has been betrayed, as has our president. Only *we* can save him and our country." Pikalov rose. "We leave at dawn."

The meeting broke up and they watched as the Valkyrie leadership left the building, only Pikalov remaining in the room. The door to the operations center hissed open and Morrison entered. Leroux turned to Tong, pointing at the ceiling. "Replay that for the Chief."

Tong complied and Morrison listened to the brief recording, the man fluent in Russian. "What the hell was that?"

"That was a meeting that just took place among the Valkyrie leadership, at least the last few minutes of it. Sherrie just placed a micro drone on the window and we were able to record it."

Morrison leaned against the workstation. "Are we talking about a coup?"

"It sort of sounds that way, though they appear to be targeting the military leadership, not the political."

Morrison scratched his chin. "There's not much of a distinction over there."

"We're going to have to warn Jack somehow."

"How do you propose to do that?"

"We have to get comms to him, at least temporarily, so we can have a conversation. We need to know what he's found out and he needs to know what we've found out."

Child cleared his throat. "But why? I mean, obviously he should be informed, but isn't a coup a good thing? I mean, don't we want the Russian president dead?"

"No, you heard it. That's not what they're talking about. They want to replace the Russian military leadership, not the president. That means hardliners. Extreme hardliners, probably. That could mean all-out war led by people who support the use of tactical nukes on the battlefield."

Morrison shook his head. "If this goes nuclear, we could be heading into World War Three. These guys have to be stopped."

Child raised a finger. "How the hell's one guy going to stop them? There are thousands there. He's just Jack."

Morrison regarded the young man. "Sometimes all it takes is one fly in the ointment."

Child grunted. "Better be one hell of a big fly."

Valkyrie Encampment, Russian-Held Territory

East of Bakhmut, Ukraine

Colonel Mikhail Bogatov spotted their freshly showered new arrival heading to the mess, apparently still hungry after his private dinner with the general. He didn't trust the man. He was too cocky. Confidence was one thing, utter arrogance another. It was just something about the way the man carried himself that set off his radar, yet he had been there when Jack, as he wanted to be called, had saved the general's life, taking two rounds to his back. He could have ducked for cover like everyone else on the security detail had, but instead, he had merely turned his back toward the gunfire and pulled Pikalov close to him, acting as a human shield.

Was it a selfless act or something else? He was wearing body armor, but that only provided so much protection. Was the man good enough to tell from the sound of the previous rounds how far the shooter was then quickly calculate that the bullets would have lost enough velocity to not penetrate? It was possible, if he was who he said he was.

Directorate Z was legendary, the best of the best, but also the most inhumane people Russia had to offer the world. They had no morals, had no rules. Things here were bad, Valkyrie a vicious organization, but even they didn't approach Directorate Z's notoriety. It was one of the reasons why he wore the balaclava everywhere, even inside. He intended to have a future after this was all done, and didn't want to be tainted by his association with Valkyrie.

He opened the door to the morgue, one of the busiest buildings at the encampment. While they were about to be victorious on the battlefield, the cost was high, and every body recovered was processed. One of their doctors, doubling now as coroner, Major Maxim Svetov, looked up from one of the corpses. Bogatov recognized it as one of those Jack had eliminated earlier, claiming they were traitors. He knew these men, though not well. He found it hard to believe there were traitors among them, but then again, was someone who betrayed a paramilitary organization really a traitor, or was that word reserved for those who betrayed their country?

Svetov acknowledged him with a wave of a gloved hand, covered in blood. "Perfect timing." He pointed at the body's back, revealed by a bright light shining overhead. "What do you make of this?"

Bogatov stepped over and peered at a wound in the man's back. "I don't know. Definitely not a gunshot."

"Agreed."

Bogatov's eyes narrowed. "Then what do you think made it?"

"If I had to guess, I'd say it was from an arrow that was later yanked out post-mortem. Did any of our people mention seeing a bow or a crossbow?"

"No."

"What about an arrow or bolt lying on the ground somewhere?"

"No, nobody mentioned anything, and I didn't see anything. Are we sure it was an arrow? It wasn't just some sort of pointed object that Jack grabbed and stuck in his back, then pulled out to use again, like a knife?"

Svetov dismissed the idea, pointing at the wound. "See the four cuts from the arrowhead? It was definitely an arrow of some sort. There's no way that was made by a knife. And besides, everyone, including this poor bastard, was shot with a Makarov nine-millimeter, probably a PMM." He tapped the pale flesh beside the wound. "This needs to be explained. If our new friend didn't do this, then someone else did. And either he's lying to us and has a partner somewhere out there, or there's another traitor who tried to silence these guys before they could talk."

Bogatov didn't like the sound of either possibility. He left the building without saying anything else and headed to the warehouse where the events of earlier had gone down. He examined the area closely but found nothing beyond pools of blood. He stood where Jack must have. He closed his eyes, recalling the scene. The victim with the apparent arrow in his back was closest to the door and had been found prone on the floor, his head toward where Jack had been standing, his boots facing the exit. It had to mean he was shot from behind by someone other than Jack.

But something didn't make sense.

Everyone killed was closer to the door than Jack was. That would have to mean he was inside the warehouse and they had entered through the door and caught him inside. And if they did, the door might have been left open. There had been a report that someone was outside the fence line earlier. Could they have fired the shot? Jack had to have had help, and the positioning of the bodies definitely meant he hadn't caught a group of traitors.

A group of loyal Valkyrie soldiers had caught a spy in their midst.

Outside the Valkyrie Encampment, Russian-Held Territory

East of Bakhmut, Ukraine

Sherrie zipped up her ghillie suit and stretched, making certain she had full range of motion before setting off toward the Valkyrie camp with the bare minimum of supplies—her crossbow, several bolts, and a sidearm. Her mission was simple. Deliver comms to Jack then get the hell out.

It sounded simple enough, however the patrols were more frequent now that her trail had been found from earlier in the day. They knew someone was out here, and like anyone, would be determined to find them.

"Control, Skylark. Report, over?"

Leroux responded. "Skylark, Control Actual. You have a gap in the patrols. You're clear to approach, over."

She dashed forward then dropped, crawling the final fifty yards, carefully watching the guard towers, those manning them more alert now than earlier. She kept inside the tree line, and prepped her crossbow. “Location of Jackrabbit?”

“He’s on the number four side, just ahead of you, leaving the mess hall. Do you have eyes on him?”

She panned to the right, toward where the mess hall was, the plans for the camp memorized. She spotted Jack leaving the mess hall and head toward the fence line where he likely suspected she would be.

“He’s clear, Skylark.”

He passed between two buildings, alone, and she loosed a bolt. It sailed through the air, embedding itself into the ground at his feet. He reached down and grabbed it, removing the small packet she had attached to it when someone stepped out of one of the buildings and rounded the corner.

Oh, shit!

Valkyrie Encampment, Russian-Held Territory

East of Bakhmut, Ukraine

"What do you have there?"

Jack resisted the reflex to flinch and instead turned, holding up the bolt. "Not sure. It just landed at my feet."

"Bullshit. You know exactly what it is," said the man, his face covered by a jawbone balaclava. He closed the gap between them, reaching for his sidearm. "You're a spy."

Jack plunged the crossbow bolt into the man's neck and twisted, blood spurting from the torn aorta. His enemy's eyes bulged as he dropped to his knees and Jack ripped off the man's mask, smirking at the sight of Colonel Mikhail Bogatov, a man on the CIA's most wanted list for being involved with the paying of bounties in exchange for the murder of American soldiers. "Well, Langley will be happy to hear you're dead, you bastard."

"I knew you were CIA," gasped Bogatov as he keeled over, the blood pumping from his neck slowing before finally coming to a halt.

Jack stuffed the balaclava in his pocket then removed the ring from the man's hand. He put it in a different pocket then rolled the body under the building and out of sight. He opened the package delivered by the bolt, finding comms gear inside. He pushed the device deep into his ear canal then pushed three times on his ear, activating it.

"Control, this is Jackrabbit. Anyone home?"

Operations Center 3, CIA Headquarters

Langley, Virginia

Leroux snapped his fingers. "Patch in Skylark."

Tong nodded, giving a thumbs-up as he fit his headset in place.

"Jackrabbit, Control Actual. We read you. Status?"

"You'll be happy to know I just killed Colonel Mikhail Bogatov. He accused me of being a spy. For the moment, I believe I'm secure, but he seemed pretty certain of himself. I'm not sure if he thought I was a spy because of the arrow you fired at my feet, or something else. Why the attempt at comms?"

"Skylark managed to listen in on the last few minutes of that meeting. It sounds like they're planning a change in leadership at the top of the military food chain. They're leaving tomorrow to take over Rostov-on-Don, across the border in Russia. It sounds like they're going to set up an HQ there, and once they're secure, they're sending a column to

Moscow that, unfortunately, was supposed to be led by the man you just took out."

Jack cursed. "Understood. I'll try to get invited to the party. So, it's not a coup attempt?"

"Negative. They appear to want to keep the president in place, and this is designed to help save him from a possible coup by others."

"Interesting. These buildings are loaded with supplies, including a shit load of ammo. All that crying on social media is a lie."

"Copy that, Jackrabbit."

"Someone is coming," hissed Tong. "You've got a hostile approaching."

"Shutting down. I can't risk being caught with this thing. Have Skylark arrange another delivery if it's necessary. I'll start doing drops if I can. Jackrabbit, out."

Valkyrie Encampment, Russian-Held Territory

East of Bakhmut, Ukraine

Jack pinched the fake hair in his ear linked to the tiny piece of gear buried in his ear canal. He pulled the device free then dropped to a knee, tossing it under the building as someone rounded the corner.

"Hey, give me a hand!"

The new arrival rushed over. "What's going on?"

"There's a body under here."

"What?" The man dropped to the ground and they both pulled Bogatov's body free.

"Do you recognize him?"

The new arrival shook his head. "No, but by the way he's dressed, I think it's Colonel Bogatov."

"Are you sure?"

"No, I've never seen him without his mask."

"Is he the one that wears that jawbone balaclava?"

"Yes."

"Holy shit! Isn't he one of the general's key commanders?"

"No one is more key."

Jack stood. "We've been betrayed. Go get the general. He needs to see this. And lock down the camp. This just happened. Whoever did this is probably still here. And whatever you do, don't tell anyone who you think it is. The general will probably want to keep this quiet if it is him."

South of the Valkyrie Encampment, Russian-Held Territory

East of Bakhmut, Ukraine

The moment Sherrie had delivered the comms package, she had fallen back from the fence line and once again used the river to make her escape. The water had been colder now that the sun had set, but her gear had kept her dry. She was now secure in her hiding place when alarms sounded in the distance. She activated her comms, the secure burst mode transmissions it used extremely difficult to detect.

"Control, Skylark. Report, over."

Leroux replied. "Looks like the camp is going ape shit. Jack had an interaction with someone and pretended to discover the body of the man he just killed."

"What are my orders?"

"Exfil north. We're arranging a rendezvous to get you back into Ukrainian-controlled territory. We might need you to follow Jack into Russia tomorrow."

"Lovely." She looked down at herself. "I'm going to need a change of clothes."

Valkyrie Encampment, Russian-Held Territory

East of Bakhmut, Ukraine

Jack stood in the morgue with Pikalov and one of the camp's doctors, Svetov, Bogatov's body quickly and quietly moved inside before anyone could recognize him.

"What do you think?" asked Pikalov, staring down at the body, the cleaned wound revealing a jagged tear.

"Something with a pointed tip," replied Svetov.

"So, a knife?"

Svetov winced, tilting his head slightly to the side before pointing at the wound. "See these four cuts? It could be another one killed by an arrow."

Jack played dumb, his eyes narrowing. "Another?"

"Yeah. One of the guys you encountered was taken out by an arrow to the back."

Jack stared at him. "Wait a minute. The one by the door?"

"I think so."

"Huh. I thought he got hit by a stray bullet or something. He came at me and just dropped as I fired. I didn't take much notice because I was dealing with the other three guys. But wouldn't the arrow have still been in him?"

"One would think, but it wasn't. It looked like it had been pulled out. Did you do it?"

Jack gave him a look. "Why the hell would I do that? And when? I called for help right away." He pointed at Bogatov. "And his arrow is missing too. Whoever did this is still here. He probably removed the arrow in the warehouse during the confusion. If we can figure out who exactly had access to the body between when he was killed and you got to him, we can narrow our suspect pool."

Pikalov cursed. "We don't have time for this. He was key. I'm going to have to shuffle things around for tomorrow's operation."

Jack faced him. "I'm not sure what's going on, but count me in. I can fill pretty much any role. I'm betting you've seen my full record by now."

"I have." Pikalov chewed his cheek for a moment. "Come with me." He turned to Svetov. "Don't tell anyone about this. If word gets out that he's dead, everyone will be thinking the man next to them is a traitor."

Russian-Held Territory

North of Bakhmut, Ukraine

Sherrie was heading northwest finally, having first headed deeper into Russian-controlled territory, putting some distance between herself and the front lines. Langley was guiding her, warning her of any patrols. She had lost count of how many times she had dove into the ditch to avoid approaching vehicles or Russian soldiers on foot, and it had taken her far too much time to cover any significant distance. Things were only going to get worse as she neared the front lines.

A woman's scream sliced through the eerie silence, screams of terror, of panic. Sherrie rushed through the trees that lined the road and found a farmhouse, a Russian jeep parked in front, two soldiers standing at the door while a man laughed inside. A smack rang out, an open hand on skin, and the woman cried out.

Sherrie's blood boiled.

She drew her sidearm, screwing a suppressor in place as she approached in the near dark. She aimed at the first Russian, holding her fire until someone noticed her, and managed to get within thirty feet before the eyes of the man she was aiming at bulged. She placed two shots in him and two more in the back of his friend. They both crumpled to the ground, their deaths going unnoticed by their partner inside, who continued to laugh and smack around the woman.

She climbed the porch steps and opened the door to see a woman, her dress torn, a knife held in her right hand, her attacker gripping her by the wrist, rendering the weapon useless as he continued to laugh at how helpless she was. Sherrie didn't bother delivering a message. She simply put two rounds in his back and he dropped in silence, releasing his victim's wrist.

The young woman stared at Sherrie in horror and confusion, then released the knife, the metal blade clattering on the tile floor.

"Are you all right?" asked Sherrie in Russian, most in this area speaking the language.

The woman nodded.

"I've killed the two outside. Can you manage them or do you need help?"

The woman shook her head. "I'll feed them to the pigs. Cannibalism."

Sherrie chuckled. "Good idea. I'm going to take their vehicle, if you don't mind. If they come here and find the bodies, tell them I was a man."

"You're more of a man than this piece of shit."

"Aw, thanks, sweetie, that's the nicest thing I've heard all day." Sherrie headed for the door. "Be safe." She stepped outside and climbed into the jeep, finding the keys in the ignition. She started the engine and pulled away, activating her comms, Leroux already jumping on her.

"Skylark, did you just kill two Russians?"

"No."

There was a pause and she smirked. "But I saw you."

"I killed three, and now I've got a ride. Where am I heading?"

Leroux sighed. "Stay on this road for now, but it's going to get bumpy. We have to send you cross-country. Your rendezvous is only a few klicks from where you are. Let's just hope your handiwork isn't discovered anytime soon."

Sherrie turned onto the road, gunning it. "I think I'll be fine, but even if I'm not, I can live with that."

Valkyrie Encampment, Russian-Held Territory

East of Bakhmut, Ukraine

Jack waited outside Pikalov's office as a search was conducted in the camp. Somebody rushed inside, two arrows gripped in his hand. He knocked urgently.

"Come!" called Pikalov from his office.

The man entered, closing the door. "We've found the arrows," he reported, the walls thin enough for Jack to hear everything.

"Where?"

"One was under the building where the body was found, and the other one, get this, was in his pocket."

"What?"

Jack cursed silently to himself. He should have hidden the arrows better, but there hadn't been time in either instance. Bogatov had obviously found the arrow he had tossed inside the warehouse before they had their encounter.

Pikalov responded to the shocking discovery with a perfectly reasonable theory. "He obviously found the first arrow, and on his way to report his discovery, was taken out by whoever this traitor is. At least it solves one part of the puzzle. Now we just need to figure out who the hell is killing our people. Get him in here."

The door opened and Jack was beckoned inside.

"You're dismissed."

The man who had found the arrows closed the door behind him, leaving Jack alone with Pikalov. He took a chance and tossed the balaclava and ring on the table.

Pikalov's eyebrows shot up. "Explain yourself!"

"I took the mask and ring when I found the body so no one would recognize him. I'm assuming because he wears that mask, no one really knows what he looks like."

It took a moment for Pikalov to recover from the shock. "No, they don't."

Jack leaned in. "Listen, I don't know what's going on here, but from what I've been able to put together, something big is happening, and I want to help." He pointed at the balaclava. "And if he's important, I've got an idea."

"What?"

"He hid his face and I never heard him speak. The soldier who helped me with the body said the same thing. Is that true?"

"It is. He spoke to me and me alone, except on rare occasions when it was absolutely necessary."

"Why?"

"His voice is known in military circles. He did a lot of social media for the military before he left and joined us. Moscow wasn't happy, so he keeps a low profile."

Jack smiled. "Then my idea just might work."

"And what is that?"

Jack picked up the ring and put it on, then tied the balaclava in place. "We continue as if nothing has happened."

Pikalov stared at him, a smile soon spreading. "It just might work, but stepping into his shoes could mean your death."

Disputed Territory

North of Bakhmut, Ukraine

Sherrie brought her commandeered vehicle to a halt and turned off the engine. The last couple of miles had been across brutal terrain, the ride rough, made all the worse by the fact she had done it with no lights. She was too close to the front lines and couldn't risk being taken out by either of the sides.

Leroux guided her. "They're a hundred meters ahead of you. Get out slowly with your hands raised. They're expecting you on foot."

"Copy that." She opened the door and slowly stepped out, closing it, then raised her hands over her head. She walked forward slowly, her eyes darting about, carefully picking her way across the rough terrain.

"Fifty meters, straight ahead."

She couldn't see anything. It was dark now. Langley would be picking them up by their heat signatures. She continued forward on faith.

"Twenty meters."

Sixty feet.

She still saw nothing. They remained hidden for the moment, which shouldn't concern her, though it did. There was no reason for them to reveal themselves, but all it would take would be an itchy trigger finger to end her life. Everyone was on edge in this entire region. Over a year of constant fighting tended to do that.

"Ten meters, straight ahead."

Thirty feet.

She stopped. "I've always thought the Moscow Symphony was overrated," she said into the darkness.

A voice responded. "I've heard the Berlin Symphony is a delight."

She smiled at the response and the half-dozen silhouettes that rose from the ground. She stepped forward, lowering her arms, and extended a hand to the Ukrainian Special Forces commander who had helped with her insertion. "Good to see you again, Major."

"And you. I didn't think we were going to ever see you again."

She shrugged. "I like to be unpredictable."

He chuckled. "Let's get the hell out of here." He gestured at the stolen rig. "Somebody's eventually going to notice that's missing and just might come looking for it."

Valkyrie Encampment, Russian-Held Territory

East of Bakhmut, Ukraine

Jack left the long briefing, his mind reeling. What he had just been told was insane, though it matched the little bit overheard by Sherrie's micro drone. But there was so much more to the plan, and unfortunately, no way to communicate it to Langley. He had to figure out a way to report what he had discovered, but how he would manage that, he didn't know.

Sherrie couldn't risk another contact. The entire camp was on high alert, and patrols were out searching for her. They didn't know they were searching for a woman, they just knew there was somebody out there. He was certain Leroux would have sent her to safety hours ago, so he was on his own.

Several Valkyrie personnel hailed him as he passed, reacting to the mask and not the man. He ignored them, as Bogatov would have, and instead entered the dead man's quarters, all senior commanders assigned their own cabin. He turned on the light, the switch by the door, and did a quick assessment while standing in front of a mirror, taking in everything without looking too obvious, just in case he was being watched. He doubted he was. Bogatov was too high in the organization. He got the sense that those who wore these rings were afforded extra privileges.

There was a knock at the door.

"Enter."

The door creaked open and a woman stepped inside wearing an ankle-length trench coat. She closed the door then opened the jacket, revealing she had been recently mugged, the thief taking her clothing.

"General Pikalov thought you might enjoy me."

Jack smiled. "General Pikalov thought right."

She let the coat drop to the ground then she slinked closer before dropping to her knees and undoing his belt. He began lifting the balaclava to remove it when she reached up, stopping him. "No, leave it on."

Jack eyed her. "What?"

"Keep the mask on. I want the legend, not the man."

Jack smirked. "Your wish is my command."

Perhaps it was best he wasn't on comms.

Operations Center 3, CIA Headquarters

Langley, Virginia

Packman grinned. "So do you think she's there to clean his quarters?"

Child spun in his chair. "She's there to clean something."

Tong gave him the stink-eye. "You're a pig."

Child shrugged. "And this is news to you?"

Leroux held up a hand, cutting them off. "Enough. I think we know why she's there and it proves he's in."

"Oh, he'll be in all right," snickered Child. He shrugged. "Sorry. You put it out there, so I had to run with it."

"Uh-huh. I'm guessing he's busy for the night, and the overheard conversation has them leaving in the morning. The twist is why was he wearing the mask."

Tong became serious. "It has to be that he's taken Bogatov's position, but with Pikalov's blessing. That gives him inside access, but means if anything goes wrong, he'll be the first they suspect."

Leroux had to agree with her assessment. "Let's get some shuteye. Tomorrow's going to be a busy day."

Valkyrie Encampment, Russian-Held Territory

East of Bakhmut, Ukraine

Jack rolled off his entertainment for the evening, gasping for air as his gift from Pikalov lay beside him in a pool of sweat, her chest heaving from the jackhammering she had demanded.

"My God, I've heard stories, but that…" She perched on her side, propping her head up as she stared at him, a smile on her face. She exhaled loudly. "That was unbelievable."

Thanks to a combination of the Operations Officer Intimate Encounters Handbook, and some innate natural talent.

She reached over, lifting the bottom of the balaclava. "Who's under there, I wonder."

He grabbed her wrist, stopping her, deciding it would be in character to remain a mystery. "Let's just stick with the legend, shall we."

She groaned then ran her hand down his chest before gripping Jack Jr. "Any chance he's still got some life in him?"

Jack grunted. “He does, but he doesn’t have time. Big day tomorrow.”

She pouted. “Just once more?”

Jack groaned as her hand attempted to influence his answer. “Fine, one more time, then you go.”

She grinned, and after another bout of intense rogering, she left without being asked, which was fine by him. As much as he would enjoy continuing to bump uglies with her all night, he had to get some rest. Tomorrow would be extremely busy. In fact, the coming days would be.

His assignment was to lead a column to Moscow, and once discovered, they wouldn’t go unopposed. He would be actively killing Russian soldiers, and if he was captured and it was discovered who he actually was, Pikalov would be right.

He would be killed, but not before a long and painful interrogation that could last months.

It meant he needed a contingency. What that might be, he wasn’t sure yet. He would sleep on it and hope for the best. He never feared death, though he always did his best not to bring it on.

Ibis Styles Warszawa Centrum Hotel

Warsaw, Poland

Sherrie sighed as she soaked in the tub of a three-star Warsaw hotel. After her exfil, she had managed to clean up somewhat, but not properly. She had mud and grit in places no woman should, but now she was squeaky clean and horny as hell. In the old days, she would have hit a bar, picked someone up, and satisfied her needs. But now she was in a committed relationship, so that was off the table. And she didn't mind that. She would rather be in love than in lust. The fact that she was in both just happened to be a bonus.

She loved Leroux with all her heart. He was the complete opposite of what she had always thought she would end up with, but there was just something about him she found irresistible. And since Jack had got him a copy of the CIA's lovemaking manual, the boy had really stepped up his game in the sack.

A tingle ran through her body, and the urge to take care of business was overwhelming. She dunked her head under the water then rose, climbing out of the tub and drying herself off. She headed for the bedroom and texted her man.

You up?

He replied a moment later. *Yes. Are you all right?*

Yep. Where are you?

At home.

Good. Get naked. I'm FaceTiming you in five.

A smiley face replied.

Valkyrie Encampment, Russian-Held Territory

East of Bakhmut, Ukraine

Jack woke and quickly did a bird bath then dressed. There was a knock at the door and he fit his balaclava in place.

"Enter."

The door opened, a private entering with his breakfast. He placed it on a table in the corner. "The general wants to see you as soon as you're done."

Jack nodded, saying nothing, and the young man left. He pulled the balaclava down around his neck then shoveled in every bite of food on offer. There was no telling when he would have a chance to eat next or even if he would have a chance to eat ever again. If this was to be his last meal on this earth, it was a pretty pathetic offering, but at least he would go with a full stomach.

He brushed his teeth, disgustingly with another man's toothbrush, then checked himself in the mirror before fitting the balaclava back in place and heading to Pikalov's office. He showed the ring to the guard, who let him in.

Pikalov smirked. "I trust you slept well."

Jack shrugged. "I had some trouble getting to sleep. Some woman kept insisting I bang her brains out."

Pikalov laughed. "She's a fun bundle, that one. She's yours if you want her."

Jack sat. "Something tells me I'll be a little busy for that kind of entertainment."

"You will be, but I'll have her brought with us and reserved for you, unless you want someone else."

"She'll do for now, but I have someone in mind for when things settle down. With your permission, I'll give her a call."

"You do that."

"When do we leave?"

Pikalov tapped his ear as engines roared to life outside. "Now. You'll ride with me. Ready?"

Jack rose. "Absolutely."

"Then let's go save our president."

Operations Center 3, CIA Headquarters

Langley, Virginia

Tong pointed. "There he is."

Everyone in the operations center watched as Jack, wearing Bogatov's jawbone mask, climbed in a command vehicle with Pikalov, a large convoy leaving the camp, thousands of men loaded into troop carriers.

CIA Analyst Supervisor David Epps, who had manned the overnight crew, waved a hand at the satellite image. "That's just the latest bunch we've found heading for Russia. It looks like Valkyrie is pulling most of their forces out of Ukraine and heading east."

"Interesting." Leroux logged into his terminal. "ETA?"

"They all appear timed to arrive at Rostov at roughly the same time, around seven AM."

"Do they have enough forces to take the city?"

"Absolutely. There's only a small contingent of Russian regulars there. The question is whether they can hold it. If the Russian Army responds, then they'll eventually lose, but not without heavy casualties on both sides."

Leroux folded his arms and leaned against his station. "The Russians can't afford to pull their experienced troops from the front lines. The Ukrainians would flood in. Best guess?"

Epps pinched his chin. "My guess is they take the city with few if any shots fired. The real question is what happens with that column they're sending north to Moscow."

"Yeah, that's what concerns me too. If Bogatov was supposed to lead it and Jack is now pretending to be him, then we have to assume he's going to be commanding the troops actually attempting the takeover. Once the Kremlin figures out what's happening, they're going to start hitting them with everything they've got. The chances of Jack and his new Valkyrie buddies reaching Moscow are slim to none."

Rostov-on-Don, Russia

Jack smiled from behind the balaclava as Pikalov waved at the crowds lining the streets, cheering their arrival. It was hard not to get caught up in the moment, and it was something he had never experienced before, nor expected to again. He felt like Buzz Aldrin must have, playing second fiddle to the crowd favorite, Neil Armstrong. Buzz knew why they were all there. It wasn't to see him, it was to see the man who had got there first. Today, they were among the last to pull into the city. Valkyrie forces had entered, secured the core of the city without resistance, then pushed out from there, taking over all government and military installations before the all-clear was sent for the general to claim victory and credit.

It was a damning indictment of the state of Russian politics. Here they were, a paramilitary force being greeted as liberators. If that didn't show the Kremlin what the public thought of their leadership, he didn't know what did.

Pikalov smiled at him. "See? Not a shot fired. The Russian Army isn't our enemy, nor are the people. Only the military leadership is." He laughed, waving at the crowds. "They love us!"

Jack had to agree with him, though a lot of the faces appeared rather neutral despite the waving arms. How much of this was staged? Valkyrie had cameras everywhere filming Pikalov's arrival. It reminded him of a staged photo op one might see in China or the ever-popular North Korea. Whenever a North Korean leader died, every single person in the country tried to get on camera wailing away in grief, but the moment those cameras were turned off, it was just another normal day of struggling to survive.

Was this any different? Greet our new masters with a smile or risk paying the price?

They continued for a few more minutes before they pulled up to the Southern Military District headquarters building. Pikalov stepped out, the crowd roaring, his men cheering. He raised his arms in triumph, his smile broad, as Jack stood by the car, his face covered with a ridiculous mask that made him appear like Skeletor. It had him wondering who was He-man, The Master of the Universe, in this scenario? Was it Pikalov or was it the Russian president?

As far as Jack was concerned, they were both evil.

They strode up the steps and into the building, the doors closing behind them, the roar of the crowd immediately silenced.

"This will be our headquarters for the operation. Are you ready to play your part?"

"I am, but just how far am I supposed to go?"

"All the way to military headquarters in Moscow."

Jack stopped and Pikalov faced him. "That's not what I mean. The army here might not be our enemy, but they will follow orders when their leaders are threatened. The Air Force will remove us from the map if they're ordered to."

Pikalov dismissed Jack's concerns with a flick of the wrist. "You're being sent with state-of-the-art air defense systems. Eliminate anyone who gets in your way."

"So, kill Russian soldiers, Russian pilots?"

"Anyone. Do whatever it takes to reach Moscow. Don't stop unless you hear from me."

Jack regarded him, wryly. "And if they take *you* out?"

Pikalov smiled. "Then avenge me."

Operations Center 3, CIA Headquarters

Langley, Virginia

Morrison entered the operations center, his eyes immediately turning to the main display, several satellite feeds plus flash alerts from the CIA, Pentagon, NSA, NATO, and others quickly scrolling by. "Where's Jack?" he asked as he joined Leroux.

Leroux rose and pointed at one of the feeds showing a column heading north. "If we're correct in our assumptions, then he's now playing the role of Bogatov. He's heading for Moscow as the commander of that column with orders to remove the military leadership."

Morrison cursed as he folded his arms. "If the Kremlin finds out it's an American operative leading them, we could end up going to war. And we still have no way to communicate with him?"

"None. And we can't risk trying to get somebody near him for some sort of drop."

"Nothing was prearranged?"

"We had no idea he'd be heading into Russia, let alone leading an assault on Moscow when we gave him the assignment to infiltrate Valkyrie."

"Drone?"

"We might be able to put a drone on the hood of his vehicle, but his driver would certainly notice. There's just no way to reach him while he's on the move."

Morrison closed his eyes and pinched the bridge of his nose. "Damn it, we need to be able to talk to him."

"If you could, what would you say?"

Morrison pursed his lips. "You know what? I haven't a damn clue. We need to know what's going on, what's the purpose of this? Does any of this tie into the buildup of Russian troops on the Belarusian border we've been watching for the past month? Does any of it have anything to do with the transfer of nukes to Belarusian control, or is this just another example of greed? I've watched a lot of Pikalov's social media posts. This is a man who loves the sound of his own voice. He's driven by his own ego. For all we know, he's doing this just to increase the number of followers he has."

Child snorted. "The dude's Kanye crazy."

Morrison cocked an eyebrow. "Kanye crazy? What the hell does that mean?"

Leroux rolled his eyes. "The fact you don't know, sir, makes everyone in this room respect you even more."

Morrison chuckled then leaned in, lowering his voice. "So then, it wouldn't be the right time to admit I actually knew who the hell he was talking about?"

"As long as you can't name the Kardashians you are still aces in my books."

Morrison tossed his head back and laughed. "Well, that, I can assure you, I have no clue about." He became serious once again, pointing at the screen. "If we do manage to reach Jack, tell him to find a way to get his ass away from that convoy before it reaches Moscow. We can't risk him being captured. We'll get the blame."

Tong spoke up. "I have a funny feeling they won't get to Moscow, sir." She tapped her keyboard, a new display appearing. "They've got incoming."

En Route to Moscow, Russia

Jack rode in the front of the command vehicle, marveling at just how easy things had gone so far. They had encountered no resistance, the massive column of almost 8,000 troops an impressive sight that extended for miles in either direction. Word was spreading across social media about their mission, and curious onlookers lined the road when they neared towns or cities, all of which they avoided where possible. They had one mission.

Reach Moscow.

The window to the rear slid open, one of the techs in the back monitoring their equipment calling to him. "Sir, we've got inbound choppers. Their commander is ordering us to stand down."

Jack tensed. This was it. As soon as he gave the order, there was probably no returning from this. Right now, they were a sideshow, a nuisance, but so far they hadn't killed a single Russian. It was just bluster coming from Pikalov, publicly announcing on social media exactly what they were doing. It was no secret that this convoy was heading for Moscow, and it was no secret what their mission was—to remove the military leadership that had failed the Russian Army in Ukraine.

He was well aware of why Pikalov was being so public. They didn't want the Kremlin to think they were coming for the president. This had nothing to do with the political leadership, only the military leadership, and with the friendship between the president and Pikalov well known, he had no doubt there was some level of communication between the two, perhaps even today.

"What are your orders, sir?"

Jack didn't hesitate. He couldn't hesitate. He was playing a character. "Take them out."

"Sir?"

He could hear the hesitation in his subordinate's voice. The Russian Army was their ally. Most here had once served in it. These were their comrades. "You heard me. Take them out."

"Umm, yes, sir."

Jack twisted and stared the man in the eyes. "And major?"

"Yes, sir?"

"That's the last time I repeat an order."

The man gulped. "Yes, sir."

Jack faced forward, staring out the windshield as the order was given behind him. A Pantsir-S1 mobile anti-aircraft missile platform pulled to the side of the road and came to a halt, the convoy slowing. A moment later, two missiles launched, racing into the sky before angling toward their targets. There was a flash on the horizon, then another, and Jack's heart sank. People were dead because he had ordered it. He had killed before. He had killed a lot of people in his career, but typically, it wasn't an order given by him. He simply did the killing himself. Here he had ordered somebody to press a button. He never even saw their faces. They were simply helicopter crews, perhaps a reaction force just doing their jobs, defending their country. The Russian people weren't America's enemy. It was their leadership.

Yet he still had to play a part.

"Is my sky clear?"

"Yes, sir."

"Then let's keep it that way."

Southern Military District Headquarters

Rostov-on-Don, Russia

Pikalov stood at the second-floor window, staring out at the courtyard below, now a staging area for his troops. He had over 5,000 men here now, and more were arriving. They could hold out for a hell of a long time if they had to, but that wasn't the plan. It wouldn't be necessary. Right now, everything was going exactly as he had predicted, and he couldn't help but continue to smile at the people on the streets cheering on his men.

It was an intoxicating feeling.

Today, he was a liberator, not a conqueror. And he wondered if this was how Patton felt riding into Messina, de Gaulle in Paris. Had they felt the exhilaration he now felt? Had their hearts pounded? Had they experienced the butterflies in their stomach like he had? He couldn't be sure, but one thing he did know was that he loved it. To be worshiped, to be loved by strangers, it was a form of ecstasy he could have never imagined, and he wanted to feel it again.

It was time to go out and meet his people, to post on Telegram to his followers, to revel in what he had created.

There was a knock at the door.

"Come!"

Chekalov entered. "Sir, I just thought you should know. The convoy has encountered resistance."

"What kind?

"Two choppers closed in on their position, ordering them to stand down. Bogatov had them eliminated."

Pikalov cursed. "They weren't supposed to resist."

Chekalov's eyes narrowed. "Sir?"

Pikalov waved him off. "Nothing. Keep me informed."

Chekalov left and Pikalov strode over to his desk, grabbing the satellite phone sitting on it, and dialed. "This is Pikalov. I need to speak to him."

"One moment, please."

There was a clicking sound. "Yes?"

Pikalov's heart raced. "Mr. President, we have a problem."

Operations Center 3, CIA Headquarters

Langley, Virginia

Leroux sat at his station, monitoring the reports. Sherrie was safe for the moment, which was a great comfort, but his stomach was flipping over Jack. Two choppers were down, and they were beginning to encounter resistance on the ground. There was no way he could see Jack surviving the entire trip to Moscow. The resistance would grow stiffer the closer they got, and eventually the military would stop toying with them. Air defense systems worked great against helicopters and aircraft, but send a few cruise missiles in and this was over.

He got the sense the Russians were holding back, recognizing the popularity of Valkyrie among their population. But the longer this continued, the more it threatened the political leadership. It gave the impression the president didn't have control over his own country.

Tong turned. "Sir, we just got a flash from the Pentagon."

Leroux leaned back. "What's it say?"

"The Russian troops that have been building up along the Belarusian border appear to be mobilizing."

Leroux closed his eyes and cursed. "Are the Belarusians responding?"

"Negative."

"Would they have any way of knowing?" asked Child. "It's not like they have satellites. And they wouldn't dare send any type of reconnaissance into Russian airspace. They're supposed to be allies."

Leroux concurred. "No, they wouldn't know unless they had some sort of human intelligence on the ground."

Tong leaned forward, resting her elbows on her knees. "Could it just be troop movements? They're finally committing their northern forces to the war? They'll head through Belarusian territory, reopen the northern front, make a push for Kyiv?"

Leroux sighed. "Anything's possible. Either way, whatever's happening. It's never good when Russia moves troops around. People tend to die."

En Route to Moscow, Russia

Jack fired his AK-47 through the open side window as the column continued to push forward. A rocket platform stopped on the side of the road fired over a dozen missiles in rapid succession, the warheads screaming over the battlefield, hitting their target a couple of miles ahead. Explosion after explosion erupted, smoke and flame billowing into the sky, secondary explosions following indicating their targets had been found.

The lead vehicle had reported a roadblock, light armored vehicles with about twenty troops. The order had been given by him to clear it. The moment they had come to a halt, they were set upon by several dozen Russian regulars, hiding in the trees, bordering the highway. The poor bastards didn't stand a chance. Moscow had sent these kids on a suicide mission. He had almost 8,000 men under his command, all heavily armed, all hardened by battle, most of them former Spetsnaz. A ragtag group of Russian regulars, normally assigned to some insignificant post, had no business taking on a force like this.

He fired into the tree line, intentionally hitting the ground. He had no desire to kill these soldiers, though he couldn't stop the others from doing so. He had to do what Bogatov would do, and Bogatov would order them all slaughtered.

The major in the back interrupted his thoughts. "Sir, we've got more inbound. Looks like fighter jets."

Moscow was ramping up its response. First helicopters, then a roadblock, now jets. He couldn't hesitate to see what they were doing. "Take them out." Missiles launched from behind him, streaking high into the sky before changing course as they acquired their targets. He continued to fire at the scattering Russian regulars, putting the fear of God into them, hoping they would fall back before Valkyrie forces took them out. These were just regular soldiers doing their job, defending their own country, following orders given to them by their leaders. Most of them were just kids, and besides that, he wasn't here to start a war.

Two explosions flashed in the sky above. He paused. As much as he was attempting to avoid death on the ground, there was nothing he could do about what was happening overhead, and if the Russians continued to ramp up their resistance, the casualties would continue to mount. And eventually, when it became clear they intended to enter Moscow, this farce would be over in moments. All it would take would be a few cruise missiles. The thought had him wondering why the hell Moscow hadn't launched against them yet. Pikalov had already announced what their plan was. The world knew, so Moscow had to know.

Why were they still alive?

Operations Center 3, CIA Headquarters

Langley, Virginia

Leroux rose as Morrison entered the fully staffed operations center, the room buzzing with activity as this was the center of the CIA's response to the Russian crisis. It was organized chaos.

"Report."

"Sir, Moscow is on full alert." Leroux gestured at the screen, several live newsfeeds playing showing military and police setting up roadblocks around the city and key installations. "Police and reserve units are deploying, and security at the Kremlin and all government facilities is being beefed up. It looks like Moscow is finally starting to take this seriously."

Morrison joined him, staring at the screens. "And where's our glorious Russian leader?"

"Still at the Kremlin."

Morrison cocked an eyebrow. "Why the hell haven't they evacuated him?"

Child spun in his chair. "Maybe they want to let him get killed?"

Morrison grunted. "If that's the case, then the world's already in a shitload of trouble."

Tong dismissed Child's theory. "But didn't Pikalov say they were attempting to replace the military leadership, not the president? Maybe he knows that, so he's not concerned for his own safety."

"Yes, but do you trust him to stop there?"

Tong frowned. "After recent events, I've learned not to trust most people." She waved a hand. "Present company excluded, of course."

Leroux and Morrison both bowed then chuckled at each other. Morrison held up a hand. "Sorry, Sonya, I in no way meant to trivialize what happened to you."

She shrugged. "Don't worry, sir. I know you weren't. It's better to be able to laugh at these things, otherwise you go crazy."

"Agreed." Morrison wagged a finger at the screen as the satellite zoomed in on two airframes that had just been shot down. "This has been going on too long. All they need to do is launch a few cruise missiles and take them out."

Leroux pinched his chin. "That's exactly what I was thinking. There's something else going on here. The Russian response doesn't make sense."

Ibis Styles Warszawa Centrum Hotel

Warsaw, Poland

Sherrie picked at her dinner of *kotlety mielone* and perogies, her eyes glued to the television, watching the shocking events unfolding in Russia while flash updates continued to pour into her laptop with classified intel the newscasters would kill to have access to. Jack, pretending to be Bogatov with the obvious blessing of Pikalov, was leading the column that continued inexorably toward Moscow with the ultimate objective of taking down the military leadership that Pikalov blamed for the failures in Ukraine.

It was a shocking turn of events in more ways than one. The fact it was an American CIA operative leading the charge, something known to only a few people in the world, was shocking enough. But to see a rebellion in Russia was terrifying.

Yet it still didn't make sense to her, nor apparently to the brain trust at Langley. Why hadn't the Russian military simply taken out the convoy with cruise missiles? They had tried helicopters, they had tried planes, but the state-of-the-art anti-aircraft systems, ironically supplied by the Russian military to the Valkyrie forces, had successfully foiled those attempts. According to Langley, the column had smashed through six separate roadblocks, leaving nothing but carnage behind. And if the Russian response didn't grow in seriousness, there would be no stopping Jack and the nearly 8,000 troops he commanded.

She shook her head at a fresh update. What the hell was he going to do if he actually gets there? There's no way an American could lead an attack on Russian military headquarters. If they managed to identify who he was, there was no telling what it would do to Russian-American relations. And she agreed with the latest assessment that had come from Leroux's team. While Pikalov continued to claim their target was the military leadership, could he be trusted to stop there if he succeeded? Could his thirst for power be stopped?

She had no doubt Jack would stop at some point, somehow extricate himself from the situation, but that might not matter. She pushed her plate aside, her appetite lost. If 8,000 well-armed Valkyrie troops managed to take out the Russian military leadership, whoever was in command might decide to clean house at the Kremlin as well, and Russia could be plunged into civil war, something that had never happened to a nation with a nuclear arsenal. And if the wrong people got their hands on those weapons, they could be looking at World War III.

She turned the volume up as the Russian president appeared on the screen, her stomach churning at what was about to be said.

It could mean Jack's death.

Southern Military District Headquarters

Rostov-on-Don, Russia

Pikalov sat in a rather comfortable high-backed chair, his senior commanders occupying other chairs and couches as they all watched the television screen, disbelief on most of the faces in the room at what their president had just said.

He had condemned them as traitors.

A horribly hurtful sentiment to these men, everyone here a patriot who didn't blame the president for the country's predicament, but the military leaders failing him.

Chekalov cursed as the broadcast ended. "I thought he was supposed to be on our side. What do we do now?"

The room turned toward Pikalov, confusion and betrayal written on the faces, all now staring at him. "Nothing. We stick to the plan."

"But what about Bogatov and his men? They're sitting ducks."

Pikalov held up a hand, calming Chekalov. "Trust me, those cowards in Moscow won't dare hit them like they should, which is exactly why we need to replace them. If the right people were in charge, they would have taken out our column the moment they detected it."

Chekalov sighed, shaking his head as he fell back in his chair. "Well, let's hope they don't grow some balls in the next few hours, or our people are dead."

One of his senior officers leaned forward. "Forget that. What do we do now that the president isn't on our side? Succeed or fail, we need his support. Otherwise, this all goes wrong in a bad way, very fast."

Pikalov smiled reassuringly. "Trust me, if we succeed, he'll be on our side. There's a very delicate game being played here. Remember, he's surrounded by those we intend to replace. He can't express any type of support until we're there to protect him. Once Bogatov reaches Moscow and takes over the military leadership, the president will be on that same TV within the hour, expressing his support and thanks for what we've done. Valkyrie will go down in history as the group that saved Mother Russia from the traitorous actions of a corrupt military leadership. And once things are made right, we will be victorious as a nation."

Chekalov reached forward and grabbed a bottle of vodka off the table, raising it high. "I'll drink to that!" A round of cheers broke out as he took a long swig before handing the bottle to the man next to him.

Pikalov let it make the rounds, taking the final swig himself before rising. Everyone shot to their feet. "To victory, gentlemen! Now, everyone out. I've got a call to make."

His men filed out of the room and he put the bottle back on the table then walked over to the comms gear set up in the corner. Everything was going exactly to plan, even if his men thought it was all falling apart. They would be victorious.

Just not in the way the others had thought.

En Route to Moscow, Russia

Jack had to admit he was getting caught up in the excitement of the situation. If he were leading thousands of ruthless mercenaries toward Paris, he would feel quite different, but this was Russia and his target was Moscow. This was the enemy, and besting them repeatedly was intoxicating. The plan being executed was intricate, far more than a simple push north. Groups of his column had taken over cities, military bases, and various other installations along their path, all designed to limit any possible military response. The orders were automatically transmitted from his command-and-control vehicle, the major in the back following the plan exactly, merely confirming each order with Jack before it was delivered.

He did little but deal with the unexpected.

The major passed a satphone up to him. "It's the general."

Speaking of the unexpected.

Jack's eyebrows rose slightly. He took the phone, pressing it to his ear as they rolled through yet another failed attempt to stop their advance. "Yes, General?"

"I want you to hold your position."

Jack's eyebrows climbed all the way up his forehead. "Sir, if we do, we're sitting ducks."

"Stop the column and tune into a local news station. An announcement is about to be made."

Jack covered the microphone and twisted it around. "Order the column to stop."

"Sir?"

"You heard me."

"Yes, sir." The major issued the order as his driver took his foot off the gas.

"What kind of announcement?"

"You'll see. Just hold your position and await further orders."

"Understood."

The call ended and Jack handed the phone back. The driver brought them to a halt then faced him. "What's going on, sir?"

"I don't know." Jack gestured at the radio. "Get me a local news station. The general says an announcement is about to be made." He turned back to the major. "Let everyone else know to tune in to local news. Some announcement is about to be made that's going to explain why we just stopped."

"Yes, sir."

Everyone turned their attention to the radio as the driver flipped through the stations, finally settling on one with an overly excited news anchor speaking at a mile a minute. The man was obviously on edge with everything happening in Russia. Too often, when there was a change in leadership, there was a change in those who reported on the news. Depending on how things turned out, this poor bastard might be wondering if he would live to see his family tonight.

Jack didn't have a lot of sympathy.

There was no free press in Russia. Not anymore. Those who reported on the news knew that most of what they said were lies. Yet they continued to do their job. He didn't expect them to rebel. That wasn't for most people. But character could be shown in other ways, like quitting the job and doing something else. If there was nobody left to report the news, then the lies were that much more difficult to spread.

"Wait a moment. All right, we're going to break away from this broadcast to Minsk, where the Belarusian president is about to make an announcement."

Jack cocked an eyebrow as did the driver, the implication probably lost on most who lived in the West. CNN or Fox breaking away to report on an address by another country's leader would seem routine. But with the news strictly controlled by the Kremlin, the fact they were broadcasting the Belarusian leader's speech meant they knew exactly what would be said, and everything they were about to hear had already been vetted by Moscow.

And as the man spoke, Jack had no doubt the speech hadn't just been vetted by Moscow, it had been written by them.

And it had him wondering just what the hell was going on.

Operations Center 3, CIA Headquarters

Langley, Virginia

Leroux's jaw dropped as he stared at Tong, removing his headset, everyone listening intently to the translation provided by a CIA translator. The speech had just finished, the Belarusian president taking no questions as he walked away from the podium.

Leroux turned to Packman. "Get me the official transcript."

"Yes, sir."

Leroux faced Tong. "Did I just hear what I think I heard?"

She shrugged. "If you mean that Valkyrie is being forgiven and being granted exile in Belarus with the blessing of its president and the Russian president, then yeah."

Leroux ran his fingers through his hair. "So, I did hear what I thought. How in the hell does something like that get arranged within just hours?"

"It doesn't."

Child eyed Tong. "What are you saying?"

"I'm saying that there's more going on here than we're aware of."

"Like what?"

"No idea. But we need to figure this out."

Leroux agreed. "This coup was all for show. They should have been blown to shit within the first hour. But instead, they were engaged only by equipment they could defend against. Then the Belarusian president, within hours of this all starting, announces a peace plan where they can take refuge in his country? A peace plan negotiated by him with Moscow and Valkyrie leadership? No, there's more going on here."

Tong brought up a satellite shot showing a massive military base. "Not to mention that the country they're going to take refuge in just happens to have been building this new military base only a couple hundred klicks from the Ukrainian border. A base where we know Valkyrie personnel have been spotted supervising the build."

Child's eyes shot wide. "Wait a minute. Do you think that was the plan all along? I mean, holy shit! That kind of makes sense. This was all done under the guise of getting Valkyrie troops into that base. But why?"

Leroux shook his head. "I have no idea. Let's get Sherrie into Belarus. I want eyes I can trust in there."

Ibis Styles Warszawa Centrum Hotel

Warsaw, Poland

Sherrie sipped on her water, watching the speech replayed on a local Polish station, the expert talking heads as shocked as she was. None of what was happening made sense. Valkyrie forces all over the region had abandoned their positions and converged on the city of Rostov-on-Don, greeted as liberators. Then a column was sent north, barely challenged in the grand scheme of things before being stopped only hours later with a peace plan negotiated by a Moscow puppet, announcing an end to the hostilities and exile to a willing Belarus. No one to be punished.

It was insane and it was clearly staged.

The only people it wouldn't be obvious to would be the people who came up with it, so used to lying to the masses they no longer realized how obvious their lies were to those accustomed to the truth. Unfortunately, it still revealed nothing of what the ultimate plan was. The base, southeast of Minsk, had been under construction for months. The last report she had read indicated it was capable of holding over 15,000 troops, enough to hold the bulk of the Valkyrie forces involved in today's actions. The Russians had troops along the Belarusian border and they were gearing up. Why? And then there was still what had started this whole thing. The nukes. Did they tie into this somehow?

Her comms squawked in her ear. "Skylark, Control Actual, come in, over."

Leroux's voice sent a tingle through her. "This is Skylark, go ahead."

"We need you in Belarus ASAP. Something is going on and we need your eyes there."

"I had a feeling you'd be calling."

"So, you saw the press conference?"

"You mean the Belarusian president reading the approved script from the Kremlin?"

Leroux chuckled. "That would be the one. What do you think?"

"I think the whole damn thing is scripted. Not just his speech. There's no way in hell a truce is negotiated that quickly with a base for them to take refuge in under construction for months. You'd have to be a fool to believe any of that."

"That's the assessment here as well."

"Any word on Jack?"

"Nothing. We still have no way to communicate with him though we do have eyes on him. The column he's leading is now redirecting to Belarus. We're assuming they're heading for the base they've been building."

"Like I said, rather convenient. If this isn't staged, I don't know what is."

Leroux agreed. "From beginning to end. The question is, why?"

"Any theories?"

"Only terrifying ones. We've got a staged coup and an impossible-to-believe truce that has Valkyrie troops heading for a base already built for them in southern Belarus, Russian troops building up on the border, and nuclear missiles transferred to Belarusian control."

Sherrie bit her lip. "You don't think that last bit is connected, do you?"

Leroux sighed. "If it is, then God help us all."

Approaching Russia-Belarus Border

Russia

It had been a remarkable 24 hours, and Jack was quite surprised to still be alive. His plan all along had been to immediately jump out of his vehicle no matter how fast it was going the moment the first bomb hit the column, and just make a run for it. With his luck, the first bomb would have landed squarely on his position, but there was still a chance that he might get lucky and the front of the column would have been hit first.

Fortunately, his luck hadn't needed to be tested, this farce of a truce saving all their lives. What was evident to him from all the questions from those he was sharing space with was that this was a surprise to everyone. If it was staged like he suspected, the troops didn't know. The question was, who besides Pikalov had been aware? Had the real Bogatov known that he was never meant to reach Moscow? Was that why Pikalov had let Jack lead the column despite how critically important it was?

He had thought it remarkably easy to gain the man's trust and to be given such an important mission, but perhaps he had been played all along. The mission was never important. It just needed a figurehead, and a man wearing a mask fit the bill.

The convoy slowed and Jack checked the GPS. "Looks like we've reached our new home."

The driver spat out the window. "I'm Russian. Belarus will never be my home."

"Amen to that," shouted the major from the back. "As soon as things have settled down, I'm out of here."

"Me too," agreed the driver.

Jack remained in character. "Stow that talk. We'll see what the general has to say. I'm sure he's got plans beyond sitting in this godforsaken shit hole for the rest of his years."

The driver's head bobbed. "You're right. He has to have a plan."

The convoy rolled forward again and they were waved through the border.

"The convoy lead is reporting that we have a Belarusian military escort. Four jeeps," said the major.

"Understood. Tell them to follow."

"Yes, sir."

Jack peered out the window as they crossed into Belarus, his mind racing as he struggled to figure out what was going on. The radio, government-controlled, was reporting this as a great victory for the Russian president and covering up how close they had gotten to Moscow and how many had died in the process. It was an event already being whitewashed from the record. By tomorrow, there would be no mention of it and soon any reference to it would be denied.

Then the arrests would happen for those who continued to question the official line.

But he still had no idea what was going on. The coup was obviously staged, of that he had no doubt. It was likely why Pikalov hadn't been concerned about handing control to him. He had to somehow establish comms with Langley. They had to know more than he did about what was going on. Whatever it was had to be huge because there was no way in hell you went to this much trouble just to relocate a small army to then just sit and enjoy a freshly built base.

Hotel Victoria

Minsk, Belarus

Sherrie lay on a far too lumpy bed, the hotel in Minsk horrible compared to the one in Warsaw. As soon as you entered a former Soviet Republic, you had to lower your expectations. Warsaw had once been part of the Warsaw Pact, but it was now a modern European city with amenities much closer to Western European standards. Minsk was a shit hole, the capital of a totalitarian state led by the same man for nearly twenty years while the modern world passed it by.

There was a lack of pride here. The hotel was clean, it was well maintained, but the amenities were lacking. She was not sleeping well tonight.

There was a knock at the door and she rolled off the bed. She peered through the peephole to see a man standing there, his photo already having been sent to her by Langley. She opened the door and he held up a large, insulated bag, a local food delivery service logo on the side.

"I've got your delivery."

She smiled. "Come on in. You can put it on the table just over here."

He stepped inside and she closed the door behind him as he headed for the bed. He unzipped the bag and emptied the contents then closed it back up. "Enjoy."

"I'll try."

He left without saying another word. There was nothing to be said. He was from Minsk Station, but she had full comms with Langley, so anything that needed to be conveyed would be delivered directly into her ear. What had been said was just in case they were being listened to or watched. She grabbed the scanner off the bed and activated it, pairing her phone with it, all the while making everything appear innocent just in case the jammer in the bag wasn't working properly. She would have no way to explain a bed filled with weapons and tools of the trade. If her scan showed an active camera, she might have time to escape before the authorities knocked down her door, but not much.

She slowly circled the room, searching for any evidence of listening devices, but found none. The room was clean. She disabled the jammer and ran another scan before inventorying the gear. Satisfied, she did one final scan then connected to Langley. "Control, Skylark, come in, over."

"Go ahead, Skylark."

"The room is clean. Any updates?"

"Jack just crossed the border. It still looks like they're heading for the new base."

"And Pikalov?"

"He's disappeared. Nobody has any idea where he is."

"That can't be good, or is it just part of the plan?"

"With everything I've seen so far, I'd say it's all part of the plan. I don't think he has any reason to go into hiding."

"And what about those troops sitting near the border?"

"They're still activating. For what, we don't know."

"What do you need from me?"

"There's a small town outside that base. We want you to get there and try to figure out a way to establish comms with Jack. At a minimum, we need to get ears on that base. Eyes from above aren't gonna be enough."

Belarus Army/Valkyrie Base Asipovichy

Outside Asipovichy, Belarus

Jack rolled through the gates of the massive base. Scores of wood-framed buildings, along with hundreds of large tents stretched as far as the eye could see. The facility had been under construction for months and they had spotted several Valkyrie personnel on the site, which had raised suspicions back at Langley. But now all doubt could be removed. This base had always been meant for Valkyrie, so whatever had been happening over the past couple of days had been planned for some time.

Pikalov's actions yesterday weren't him acting on a whim, nor independently. At a minimum, the Belarusians knew at least in part what was going on. He was willing to bet their knowledge was minimal. Most likely, Moscow had instructed them to build the base without telling them why. Now the question was why? Before he had gone incommunicado, he had read the reports about the Russian military buildup on the Belarusian border. It had to be related to this somehow.

His original assignment was to observe the installation of the nuclear weapons transferred from Russian to Belarusian control, and he was well aware that one of those installations was less than an hour from here. Was that just a coincidence or was this all related? And if it was, how?

They were guided deeper into the base, Valkyrie personnel already on site confidently directing each vehicle, his own sent deeper, where they were eventually pointed to a parking spot in front of a large wooden structure, black writing on an army green background indicating it was the headquarters.

He stepped out and stretched, his ass killing him, his back not much better. He was exhausted, as they all were. They had spent hours yesterday fighting their way north, which was tiring in itself, but it had been nearly 24 hours of constant driving, only stopping to refuel, that caused the real pain. These trucks, transports, and mobile weapons systems were not built for comfort, they were built for utility. All around him, men were groaning and stretching and bitching, and if it weren't for the seriousness of the situation, it would be comical.

The door to the headquarters opened and Chekalov stepped out. Jack cocked an eyebrow, surprised the man had got here before them, suggesting he had taken a much more direct route, likely by helicopter or plane. "Finally. Any problems?"

Jack shook his head, keeping his words to a minimum, maintaining his character.

"Good." Chekalov pointed to his left. "Your quarters are just down there, building C-Four, Room Six."

Jack repeated the assignment to himself.

"Get yourself cleaned up. Get some rack time, get some food, whatever." Chekalov tapped his watch. "Debrief at twenty-hundred."

Jack nodded and headed for his quarters without saying a word. He stepped inside, closing the door behind him, then giving it a quick once-over before performing a thorough examination, searching for any bugs—though not before giving an excuse for his search should there actually be one.

"Let's see if you Belarusian bastards trust us."

It appeared they did. He found nothing. Two large duffle bags sat on the bed. He unzipped them to find all of Bogatov's personal belongings inside, the same belongings he had left behind at their camp near the front lines in Ukraine. Clearly, everything had been packed up and transported here. The question was, was it before or after the announcement of their exile? He was willing to bet things were already rolling here before he had left Rostov-on-Don.

He stripped out of his clothes, threw on a robe, and headed for the showers he had spotted on his way here. He washed off two days of grime, his muscles slowly relaxing as he gave himself a moment, burying the reality of his situation if just for five minutes. He toweled off then fit the balaclava back in place as he wrapped the robe around him and returned to his quarters.

The bed was inviting, but he had caught a good chunk of sleep on the ride here. He could use a few truly restful hours on a mattress, but he had a job to do. He could sleep when he was dead, and if this turned into an exchange involving nukes, that could be soon.

He strode around the base, watching as thousands of men continued to arrive, the men already in place continuing to direct the non-stop flow, some of those already here training despite their long journey. Rows of equipment were lined up, crews going over every square inch, preparing them for battle, which had him concerned. This was supposed to be a place where they would decommission over time, reintegrate into society, disappear into the woodwork, no longer a thorn in the Kremlin's side. But that wasn't what was going on. These men were preparing for war, and from the looks of it, he was the only commander not in the loop.

And he couldn't ask why.

He was Bogatov.

He should know everything.

He would have to wait for Pikalov to arrive to get an explanation, but he had no idea when or even if that might happen. He needed to know what the hell was going on, and there was only one way he could think of to get that knowledge.

He headed for the communications hut he had located earlier.

It was time for a booty call.

En Route to Asipovichy, Belarus

Minsk Station had arranged an SUV for Sherrie, loaded with custom gear just in case the need arose. She had cleared the depressing city of Minsk, and now headed southeast toward Jack's last known position. Langley had spotted him arriving without incident, which was a relief, though the last report indicated there was heavy activity at the base, contrary to what most had expected. They were supposed to be in exile, not prepping for a mission.

Whatever was going on wasn't over.

She had to somehow make contact with Jack, though at the moment, she had no idea how she might. She doubted firing another bolt with comms attached would work a second time.

Her phone rang and she checked the call display, the device paired with the car's Bluetooth. It showed a relayed number that indicated it was Jack and he was calling her cover. She hit the button to take the call. "Hello?" she answered in Russian.

"Hey, wonder buns, how have you been?"

"Horny as hell. You?"

"You have no idea. I'm surrounded by men and all of them are in shape."

"So?"

"So, no man boobs to even fantasize about."

She laughed. "It sounds like you need some serious loving. Where are you?"

"Classified. Where are you?"

She had to assume someone might be listening. "I was visiting a friend in Minsk."

"A man?"

She grinned. "Yes, but not that kind of friend."

"I'm insanely jealous anyway."

"No need, you know you're my big man. Tell me where you are. I'll come to you. Are you at least in Europe?"

"I am. And the big boss said I could bring you in if I wanted, so I guess I'll tell you. How long would it take you to get to Asipovichy? It's southeast of Minsk."

She already knew exactly how long it would take, but that wouldn't fit the conversation. "Well, I'm just south of Minsk right now, so I'm guessing I could be there in a few hours."

"Great, get here as fast as you can. I'll give you a shout in a few and arrange a meeting. Find us a nice hotel with room service. I intend to ravage every square inch of your body for as long as I've got leave."

She squealed. "I can't wait."

Operations Center 3, CIA Headquarters

Langley, Virginia

Child regarded Leroux. "That's gotta kill you."

Leroux cocked an eyebrow. "What?"

"Hearing your main squeeze talking dirty to a guy like that."

Leroux gave him a look. "First, if she heard you call her my main squeeze, she'd crush your windpipe. Second, it's a role she's playing. Everything she says is for the benefit of those listening in. When she gets home…" He caught himself. "Well, I'm a gentleman."

Child grinned. "She bangs your brains out? You're a lucky man."

Leroux blushed, noticing Tong turning away from the conversation. He felt bad about the situation, her feelings for him still very much intact. They had both recently acknowledged their feelings, and had agreed it couldn't be, but she was still struggling.

Packman glanced at Child. "Why are you so interested in the boss' girl? I thought you had a new one of your own."

"He does!" shouted Marc Therrien from the back of the room. "Princess Leia, wasn't it?"

Child faced the much older senior analyst. "That was last night. Tonight, we're playing Cylon and Colonist. She's Athena. I'm Helo."

Morrison entered, cutting off the conversation. "Status?"

Child answered before Leroux could. "Our sex lives are good, sir."

"Pardon me?"

Snorts around the room were the response and Leroux blushed again as he rose. "Let me apologize for that. Jack and Sherrie just had a conversation where she pretended to be his girlfriend."

Morrison smiled. "Sorry I missed it."

Leroux wasn't sure how to take that, so he just continued with his status report. "They're heading for a rendezvous if he can swing it."

"Will they let him off the base?"

"I'm not sure. He seemed to think they would. At least we know he's okay and Sherrie will be there in a couple of hours."

Morrison joined him at his station, clasping his hands behind his back as he stared at the various feeds. "And still no sign of Pikalov?"

Leroux frowned. "No, he's gone completely off the grid."

"Are we sure he's alive?"

"No. But Valkyrie is modeled after a military organization, so in theory, the next in command would take over and complete whatever mission they're on."

Morrison sighed. "And we still have no idea what that is. Washington thinks they might be looking to make another major push from the north. Use Valkyrie to punch a hole through the front lines, fill it with

Belarusian troops and then Russian regulars from the divisions building on the border. Combine all that and suddenly you've got another major front that forces Ukraine to pull troops from the eastern and southern fronts. It could change the outlook for this war entirely."

"What the hell are we gonna do?" asked Child, spinning in his chair.

"All we can do is warn the Ukrainians of what might be happening and hope Jack can find out what the plan actually is, and hopefully throw enough monkey wrenches into it that the Ukrainians have a chance to prepare."

Packman folded his arms, leaning back. "Too bad we can't just bomb the shit out of the place and put an end to them once and for all."

Morrison regarded him. "Unfortunately, that would be an act of war. I doubt the powers that be would want that since Belarus and Russia have a mutual defense pact."

"So, what does that mean? World War Three if we intervene?"

Morrison turned back toward the displays showing hundreds of Valkyrie troops hard at work. "Let's hope not."

Belarus Army/ Valkyrie Base Asipovichy

Outside Asipovichy, Belarus

Jack returned the satellite phone to the rack then glanced over his shoulder to see everyone in the communications hut focused on their assigned station. He yanked two radios from the charging rack and stuffed them in his pockets before leaving. He returned to his quarters and pushed the door open slightly, peering behind it to see the towel he had dropped when he had left earlier pushed up tight against the door. If someone had entered while he was away, they would most likely have opened the door all the way, pushing the towel against the wall. Apparently, he was still trusted.

He stepped inside, closing the door behind him, then hung up the towel. He gave the room another once-over just in case, but found it clean. He tossed the two borrowed radios on his bed and sat. He turned one of them on, searching for a silent frequency, then tested it with a general call, receiving no response. It clearly wasn't actively monitored. He tuned the other radio to the same frequency then reduced the volume to zero. He tore a strip off his bedding and tied the push-to-talk button tight against the device, then tested his MacGyvered rig.

Now to plant it.

En Route to Asipovichy, Belarus

Sherrie's eyes darted over at the GPS, her route mapped out in front of her, the ETA annoyingly counting down far too slowly for her liking. She clicked the cruise control up another two KPH, bringing her to twelve over the speed limit. It was the most she could risk. If she were pulled over, she would have a hard time explaining the weapons she had, and she didn't want to kill some traffic cops just for doing their job.

She glanced at the revised arrival estimate. Only five minutes shaved off. She sighed, edging it back down. It wouldn't make enough of a difference to matter. She would get there when she got there, and according to Jack's call, he wasn't scheduled to reach out to her until almost an hour after she was due to arrive.

Her comms squawked in her ear. "Skylark, Control Actual, come in, over."

She smiled at her boyfriend's voice. "This is Skylark. Did you find me a nice romantic hotel? Jack apparently really wants to drill me tonight."

There was a pause. "You do realize I'm still your boyfriend and management reviews the transcripts."

"Don't worry. I'm sure he'll be gentle."

He groaned. "You're impossible."

"That's why you love me."

"Uh-huh."

"Hotel?"

"Yes, we found one that meets your specifications. Don't expect the Ritz, more like the Shitz. It is Belarus, after all."

She grinned, having fun at her boyfriend's expense. "Jack won't care. I'm the entertainment."

Leroux groaned again. "You're killing me, woman."

Belarus Army/Valkyrie Base Asipovichy

Outside Asipovichy, Belarus

Jack headed swiftly to the headquarters, showing his ring to the guard who immediately stepped aside and let him in. He was surprised to find a meeting in full swing, the room filled with senior commanders, most of whom he recognized.

Chekalov stopped the meeting, staring at him. "What are you doing here?"

Jack cocked an eyebrow but said nothing, remaining in character, instead sitting in a chair against the wall, surreptitiously slipping the activated radio behind the bookshelf.

"You're not needed in this meeting."

Jack held up a fist with the ring.

Chekalov dismissed the gesture. "Doesn't matter. The general says he'll brief you personally when he gets here. Until then, he wants you to relax. You've done enough." He smirked. "He said to arrange some entertainment for yourself and report back at oh-eight-hundred tomorrow."

Jack rose as the room laughed.

"Take pictures!"

"To hell with pictures! Take video!"

Jack gave a double thumbs-up and left the room to good-natured catcalls, his cover clearly still intact. He headed back to his quarters at a brisk pace. He didn't want to miss any more of the meeting than he had to. Whatever was going on was definitely not over.

The question was, why was he being left out?

En Route to Asipovichy, Belarus

Sherrie cursed as she remained stuck in a long line of cars, Langley having reported a checkpoint ahead. There was no way to avoid it. The Belarusians had placed police vehicles miles ahead, watching for anyone pulling U-turns. If she attempted to avoid the roadblock, she would just be pulled over and her car torn apart. But with each passing minute, her estimated arrival time continued to tick up.

There was nothing she could do about it, so she instead tuned in to a local pop station and cranked up the volume to fit her cover of a girl out to have a good time, not an American spy out to meet up with her partner embedded deep inside a paramilitary force that had just attempted a coup in Russia the day before.

She slowly passed a burnt-out wreck pushed off the road, and wondered what had happened to what she recognized as a notoriously unreliable British sportscar. Its damage appeared old, at least a couple of years. It appeared to have been abandoned by its owner, likely after one breakdown too many. She wondered if the car caught fire, or if the owner torched it.

Both were equally possible.

She was approaching the checkpoint now. She glanced down to make sure the girls were on display, then fluffed her long blond hair. She rolled down her window.

"Papers."

She handed over her ID supplied by Minsk Station, flashing a smile. "Busy day?" She leaned out the window slightly.

The guard's eyes bulged at the sight. "Um, every day is busy."

She smirked, squeezing her arms slightly together, improving the view. "But some are more pleasant than others?"

He smiled. "Now that you mention it."

She jutted her chin down the road. "Listen, I'm heading to Asipovichy. Do you know where a girl can have a good time there?"

His face brightened. "I'm from Asipovichy!"

"Really? You're a long way from home."

He shrugged. "It's the job. I'm heading home this weekend."

She smiled. "Well, I might still be there. Why don't you look me up when you get back home?"

He groaned, holding up his hand, revealing a wedding band she had already spotted. "If only I weren't married."

She took his hand and placed his ring finger in her mouth, flicking her tongue over the band. "It's a ring, not a lock."

He gulped, handing back her papers. "You'd better get out of here before I break my wedding vows."

She patted his cheek. “You’re a good man.”

He sighed heavily. “Yeah, sometimes I hate that.”

Belarus Army/ Valkyrie Base Asipovichy

Outside Asipovichy, Belarus

Jack held the second half of his makeshift listening device to his ear, the volume low. He couldn't risk anyone passing outside hearing the radio through the paper-thin walls. For the moment, his makeshift bug still went undiscovered. Unfortunately, he still wasn't clear on what was going on. All he had gleaned was that tomorrow morning they would be attacking something called Point Omega.

"When is the general arriving?" asked someone.

Jack recognized the respondent as Chekalov. "He's in Moscow meeting with the president. He'll be commanding from there. This is a simple operation. We'll overwhelm them like we did in Rostov. Casualties on their side should be light, but we need to make sure we minimize Russian Army casualties. The president wasn't happy with the numbers killed in our push to Moscow."

"That's Bogatov being Bogatov. Why isn't he here?"

"I'm not sure, but the general made it clear he's to be left out of the loop until he speaks to him personally tomorrow."

"But he's one of our best commanders. I thought he was always supposed to lead this."

"Not anymore."

"And we don't know why?"

"No, and that's enough talk about it. Prepare your men. Tomorrow morning we leave, and by tomorrow night, we'll have changed the course of history. Russia will be restored to its former glory and the world will once again tremble at our feet."

The sounds of the meeting breaking up had Jack turning off the radio, his mind racing. What the hell was going on? An attack was happening tomorrow, but where the hell was Point Omega, and what could be there that could restore Russia to its former perceived glory, a long-held desire of the Russian president? None of this made sense, but there was one key piece of information revealed that was useless unless he could get it into the proper hands.

He had to make his booty call.

Gostinitsa Hotel

Asipovichy, Belarus

Sherrie lay on her hotel room bed, wearing nothing but a pair of panties. The rest of her trip had been uneventful, and she had arrived and checked in without incident. The hotel was even worse than the one in Minsk, though it was at least clean. She had the TV tuned to a Belarusian government-approved TV station. There was no free press here, so anything reported she took with a grain of salt, though as she suspected, the story of what had happened yesterday was already being buried, not a mention of it made in the latest newscast.

Before showering, she had contacted Langley for an update, though there was little to report beyond that Jack was last seen entering his assigned quarters. Russia continued to activate its troops built up along the Belarusian border, and Valkyrie personnel continued to pour into their new base. But from the looks of things, it didn't appear they would be there for long. It gave credence to the theory they were planning to open up a northern front in the war. They had to be stopped, but how?

Right now, it was Jack and her, two people against 10,000, with ineffectual leadership throughout NATO sitting on their hands, hoping for a miracle.

Her phone rang, the call display showing it was Jack calling her cover. She answered. "Hello?"

"Hey, sweet cheeks. Where are you?"

She smirked. "At the Gostinitsa Hotel, waiting for you."

"What are you wearing?"

"Lipstick, perfume, and a smile."

"Ooh, my favorite outfit. I'll be there as soon as I can. I've got until eight tomorrow morning before things get busy. Can't wait to see you."

"Same here."

"Warn the neighbors they won't be getting much sleep. I'm Austin Powers randy."

She squealed in delight. "Yeah, baby!" She ended the call, immediately contacting Langley through her secure comms. "Control, Skylark, do you read, over?"

"Affirmative, Skylark."

"I just spoke with Jackrabbit. He says he's coming to meet me at the hotel and implied that something is starting around eight tomorrow morning. Do we have any idea what that might be?"

She could hear the frustration in his response. "No. We're assuming it's a move south to open another front, but that's just pure conjecture. Hopefully Jack will have more info."

"Hopefully. Is there anything we can do to stop this?"

"No. The Ukrainians have started repositioning troops, but everything is happening too fast, and they don't have a lot to spare. Most of the personnel and equipment are focused on the east and south. Unless you and Jack can figure out something, we might be about to lose this war. And if Ukraine falls, then so does Moldova, then the Baltics, and with those troops massing, I'm guessing Belarus as well. And if NATO is busy fighting the Russians in the Baltics, then we can kiss Taiwan goodbye. The Chinese will take advantage of the situation and make their move while we're fully committed in Europe."

Sherrie's chest was tight, her stomach flipping with the blunt assessment of what might be to come. "This has to be stopped."

"Well, let's hope Jack has some idea how."

Belarus Army/Valkyrie Base Asipovichy

Outside Asipovichy, Belarus

Jack was waved through the gate, some hoots following him from behind, apparently his approved booty call common knowledge. He laughed and waved as he headed toward the small town where Sherrie was waiting. He punched the address she had given him into the GPS, finding it twenty minutes away. He took his time, though he doubted local police would dare pull him over considering the Valkyrie insignia on the doors of his signed-out car.

It wasn't long before he picked up a tail.

Somebody doesn't trust me.

It could be Valkyrie or it could be the Belarusians. Either way wasn't good, though he expected Sherrie to be prepared for this. He had hoped to toss the second radio into the ditch. By the time he got back, the batteries would be drained on the second half of his makeshift bug, and he couldn't risk leaving his half in his quarters, for he would be a prime suspect if it were discovered.

He didn't bother attempting to lose his tail. He instead led them directly to the hotel, where he parked and went inside. He crossed the lobby, his Skeletor balaclava still in place, shocking the guests. He boarded the lone elevator and those already there scrambled off before the doors closed. He laughed to himself but remained stoic on the outside. He couldn't break cover while on camera. The doors opened and he stepped out into the hall, heading for Sherrie's room. He knocked a cheery pattern and she opened the door.

Naked.

She grabbed him, giving him a big kiss as she wrapped her legs around him. He grabbed her ass, one cheek in each hand as he kissed her back, carrying her into the room, kicking the door closed behind them. Any security cameras should have caught the display, confirming the booty call.

Sherrie let him go, putting a finger to her lips. She tapped at her laptop, checking the readings, then smiled. "Okay, we can talk. The room is clear, but I've set up relays on the windows. It's broadcasting a Langley prerecording of a night-long sexual encounter with almost no talking, just grinding."

Jack grinned. "That should keep anybody who might be listening in titillated." He jerked his chin at her. "Speaking of…"

Sherrie gave a toothy smile, looking down at her tatas. "Should I get dressed?"

"Not on my account, but Chris might appreciate it."

She laughed and pointed to a nearby table. "Gifts from Langley, including a new watch."

Jack inventoried the supplies as Sherrie quickly dressed. He held up the watch, having gone far too long without his lifeline, and frowned, returning it to the table.

"Problem?"

"I can't take it. I came here without a watch. If I come back with one, it might draw attention. I can't risk it."

She battled her way into a form-fitting shirt. "Yeah, you're probably right."

Jack connected to Langley through the comms sitting on the table. "Control, this is Skylark and Jackrabbit. Do you read, over?"

Leroux responded immediately. "Affirmative, Jackrabbit. Status?"

Jack filled him in. "I was followed. Not sure by whom. Could be Valkyrie. Could be the Belarusians."

"Yeah, we picked up your tail. We believe they're local."

"So, they don't trust their new guests?"

"Looks that way. Can you blame them?"

He shrugged. "I suppose not. Do we know what's going on?"

Leroux grunted. "We were hoping you could tell us."

Jack frowned at Sherrie. "I'm not sure. I was able to overhear part of a meeting. Tomorrow morning, they're attacking some place called Point Omega. I have no idea where that is, but they said there would be Belarusian *and* Russian troops. Any ideas?"

"We'll work on it."

"Any word on Pikalov?"

"He's gone off the radar since this all went down."

"According to what I overheard, he's in Moscow meeting with the Russian president. He'll be commanding things from there."

"Interesting that he's avoiding the danger. Normally he doesn't shy away from the front lines."

Jack sat on the edge of the bed. "Yeah, I found that curious as well."

"Do they suspect anything about you?" asked Sherrie.

"I'm not sure. They've cut me out of the loop re tomorrow's op. Apparently Pikalov will be calling me. The real Bogatov was supposed to command this, and I no longer am. I get the impression that the others have no idea I'm not who I pretend to be. And if Pikalov suspected I wasn't who I said I was, he would have had me killed by now. I think I'm safe to return to the base. Besides, we don't have a choice. I have to find out what the hell's going on and figure out some way to stop it, and you guys have to figure out where Point Omega is. That's critical to figuring out what this is all about, but if we can't, if I were the Ukrainians, I'd hit this base with everything I've got before they have a chance to mobilize. It might be their only hope to not lose this war."

"Agreed," said Leroux. "Unfortunately, all we can do is make our recommendations, and the Ukrainians don't have a lot of hardware with that kind of range."

"Then NATO should do it, but we both know that's not going to happen."

Leroux agreed. "No, it's not. What's your plan?"

Jack grinned at Sherrie. "My plan is, for the moment, to sign off. We've got some heavy-duty shagging scheduled, then I need to get some sleep. Tomorrow's going to be a busy day."

Leroux groaned. "Thanks for sharing. Remember, as Control Actual, I can put a contract out on you."

Jack laughed, smirking at Sherrie. "Now *that's* love."

Operations Center 3, CIA Headquarters

Langley, Virginia

Morrison entered the operations center, slightly disheveled. Everyone had looked better. Since this ordeal had begun, no one had gone home, everyone catching sleep when they could in the temporary quarters located in the building. Apparently, the Chief was overdue. "So, you heard from Jack?"

Leroux nodded, having notified him immediately after contact had been made but not providing the details. "Yes, sir. Just got off the line with him. He's catching some rack time before tomorrow."

"What's the word?"

"Apparently, Valkyrie plans to attack some place called Point Omega. All we know about it is that it must be within range of the base, and that there are both Belarusian and Russian troops there."

"And when does this start?"

"Sometime after eight AM local, tomorrow. Bogatov was apparently supposed to command the operation but no longer is. Jack was told that Pikalov is with the Russian president and will be commanding things from there, and was supposed to talk to Jack personally at some point to explain what was going on."

"So, we're still in the dark?"

"Yes."

"What's Jack's plan beyond sleep?"

"He thinks it's safe for him to go back to the base, so that's what he intends to do unless we find out something that stops him."

Morrison dismissed the idea. "No. He needs to go back in. Right now, he's the only hope we have of stopping whatever the hell they're up to. Do we have any idea where this Point Omega is?"

Tong turned in her chair. "I've got an idea and you're not going to like it."

"What?"

"Well, Jack said it would have Russian *and* Belarusian troops. The only location anywhere near where their new base is that has troops from both countries is Yuzhny Military Base."

Morrison's eyes narrowed. "Why does that sound familiar?"

"Because it's one of the locations where the Russian nukes were transferred to."

Morrison grabbed at his hair, pulling his fingers through it. "Oh, shit." He headed for the door. "I need to inform the president. We might not be able to sit on the sidelines anymore."

Gostinitsa Hotel

Asipovichy, Belarus

"Wake up, sleepyhead."

Jack groaned and opened his eyes to find Sherrie leaning over him. He was exhausted and had fallen asleep the moment his head hit the pillow. He could use more sleep but was happy to be woken by the sexiest alarm clock he had seen in a long time. "What time is it?"

"Six AM. Get yourself cleaned up. I've ordered breakfast, and Langley wants to brief you on what they've discovered."

He stripped out of his underwear as he headed for the shower. "And what's that?" he asked, leaving the door open as he turned on the water.

"They think Point Omega is Belarus Army Base Yuzhny."

Jack cursed. "You mean where some of those Russian nukes were transferred to?"

"Exactly."

He tested the water temperature then stepped in, the water hot, the pressure crap. "If they're hitting that base with the blessing of the Russian president, it's for one of two reasons."

Sherrie leaned against the doorframe. "And those are?"

Jack lathered up the soap. "Either to steal one or more of the warheads to sell on the black market—"

She interrupted. "I don't like the sound of that. And the other?"

"To launch the nukes themselves."

Sherrie's eyes shot wide. "Why would they do that? That could lead to nuclear war."

Jack dismissed the idea. "No. Remember, these are tactical nukes, not strategic. They're meant to be launched over shorter distances and to impact the battlefield. They're lower yield."

Sherrie's eyes narrowed. "So, what are you saying?"

"My guess is they intend to launch against Ukraine. They could devastate Kyiv and a few other major population centers, and Ukraine would be forced to surrender."

"You mean like the Japanese in World War Two."

"Exactly."

"But what we now consider low-yield warheads still wiped out Hiroshima and Nagasaki."

"I know, but at least these aren't megaton yields. The Russians swoop in, blame Valkyrie for it…" He stopped, waging a finger. "Wait, they've been building up along the Belarus border, right?"

"Yes."

"Well, that's why."

"What's why?"

"They're going to invade Belarus and take it over, claiming they're doing it to stop the rogue state from launching again. When the dust settles, they have Belarus under their control and Ukraine will be a failed state they can finally conquer. NATO won't do anything because nobody involved is a member." He turned, washing the boys out of her sight.

"It's diabolical."

"It's genius."

"How do we stop it?"

He shrugged. "I don't know, but I've got to get in on that mission, because I doubt NATO is going to hit a nuke site unprovoked. That could trigger a nuclear response from Belarus that targets Western Europe."

Sherrie headed out of the bathroom. "I'm going to contact Langley and tell them your theory. This has to be stopped. Enough pussyfooting around."

Belarus Army/ Valkyrie Base Asipovichy

Outside Asipovichy, Belarus

Jack approached the gate, once again disguised as Bogatov, his balaclava back in place. He was more rested today than he had been in at least a week, and he always enjoyed spending time with a beautiful woman, even if there was no chance of a brown-chicken-brown-cow session. Sex in their trade was casual. Sometimes it was part of the mission to seduce a potential source, other times it was just stress relief, and operatives quite often hooked up just to feel human.

If Sherrie wasn't so serious about Leroux, last night might have been a lot of fun, but he respected her relationship with him and he respected the two of them too much to ever make a move. Besides, there would be no point. If he tried anything, she would tear his nuts off.

He deactivated the comms buried deep in his ear canal with a double tap, just in case he was scanned upon arrival. He was waved through and he returned the signed-out car to the carpool, reactivating his comms so Langley could listen in as a guard approached.

"Chekalov wants to see you right away, sir. He's in the briefing room at HQ."

Jack acknowledged him without saying a word and headed for the nearby building. He showed his ring and was allowed through. He entered the briefing room to find Chekalov sitting at the far end of the table with the rigged radio sitting in front of him.

"Care to explain this?"

Jack kept his cool. He walked over and picked it up. "Jerry-rigged radio, poor man's eavesdropping device. Where'd you find it?"

Chekalov jerked his chin toward the bookshelf. "Behind there, where you were sitting yesterday."

Jack cocked an eyebrow, placing the radio back on the table. "You're accusing me?"

"Can you think of someone better?"

"No, but I would suggest finding a matching radio."

"They all match. It's one of ours."

Both of Jack's eyebrows rose. "Oh? Have you accounted for them all?"

"Two are missing, this is one of them."

"And the other?"

"We haven't found it yet, and I doubt we will."

Jack regarded him. "Why's that?"

"I'm sure you disposed of it after you left last night to meet up with your partner on the outside."

Jack chuckled. "I'd hardly call her my partner. She's just a piece of ass. If you don't believe me, contact the Belarusians. They put a tail on me as soon as I left."

It was Chekalov's turn to be surprised. "They did?"

"Yes. I'm sure the general can call them to get a report on my activities. I have no doubt they were listening in somehow. They should be able to confirm that we hardly said two words to each other. I just used her like a stress relief ball, then caught some sleep, woke up, came back exactly as ordered."

Chekalov stared at him. "If only I could believe you." He whistled and the door opened, two guards stepping inside. "Lock him up. We'll let the general decide what to do with him."

Jack's eyebrows rose. "He's here?"

"No, but he'll be landing when we complete our mission."

"The mission I'm not allowed to know anything about."

"The mission I think you know everything about."

Jack dismissed the notion. "Sadly, I know nothing except that I could be a big help if you let me."

"Too risky." Chekalov flicked his wrist at the new arrivals. "Get him out of my sight, and if he tries anything, shoot to kill. Pikalov's orders."

Operations Center 3, CIA Headquarters

Langley, Virginia

Leroux watched as Jack was led from the headquarters building and Morrison cursed as he entered the operations center, catching the tail end of things.

"Is he under arrest?"

Leroux frowned. "It looks that way."

"That's an unfortunate turn of events. What happened?"

"They found the radio he had planted."

"Where's the second one?"

"He left it with Sherrie," replied Tong. "We monitored it overnight but there were no further meetings in the room before the battery died on the other end."

"It's dead?"

"Yes, sir. It was transmitting all night, so it burned through its juice."

"But he's got proper comms now?"

Leroux confirmed it. "Yes, sir. We're listening in on everything being said right now. Chekalov just ordered him locked up until Pikalov arrives later."

"Shit. That definitely takes him out of the mix."

"Any word from Washington?" asked Leroux.

"The Ukrainians have been notified of what we fear, but beyond repositioning troops already in the area, there's not much they can do. And if this goes nuclear, they lose the war. They know that. And there's no way to evacuate major population centers in time. It would just cause panic for something they're not convinced is actually happening."

"Seriously?"

Morrison shrugged. "Washington has its doubts too. No one there can believe the Russians would do this. It defies all logic."

Leroux disagreed. "Not really. Jack has a theory, and my gut tells me he might be right."

"Oh? And what's this theory?"

"Think about it. They stage the coup, Belarus steps in and says you can stay with us at our shiny new base we just happen to have built near the Ukrainian border and near our base where some of these new nukes are sitting. That gets Valkyrie there en masse with the world left none the wiser. The Russians put troops on the Belarus border. Valkyrie attacks the base, takes the nukes, and launches them. They have the codes because the Russians gave them to them. Ukraine is hit, Belarus is blamed, and if not them, then an out-of-control Valkyrie. Ukraine surrenders as morale collapses along with their command structure. Russian troops pour into Belarus to take back their nukes, and NATO lets them, perhaps bombing the shit out of their military installations as punishment.

"In the end, Russia has Belarus and Ukraine. They can then move quickly on Moldova, perhaps the rest of Georgia. The question then is what do they do next? Do they retake the Baltics with nuclear horror playing out on the TV screens? Will NATO honor Article Five or will NATO crumble? And if there's any hesitation, China might take the opportunity to make their move once and for all on Taiwan. Do we honor our commitment to defend them? This is domino theory all over again. If they succeed today, Russia could retake a good chunk of the former Soviet Union within days, and China could reunite their country after over seventy years."

Morrison stared at Leroux in disbelief. "It's a terrifying notion, but I think you're right. I've been pushing Washington, but they don't want to strike first." He pointed at the screen. "Any indication of a launch, you let me know. That might push them over the fence."

Leroux cleared his throat, hesitating.

"What is it?"

"Well, there's one thing we might be able to do."

"What's that?"

"Tell the Belarusians what's about to happen."

"You don't think they know?"

"Well, it would at least answer the question of whether they do."

"How?"

"If they react, that means they realize they've been set up as a patsy. If they don't, then they were willing participants and deserve whatever happens to them."

Morrison scratched at his chin. "Interesting thought. I'll run it by Washington."

"Tell them time is of the essence. Those Valkyrie troops are leaving their base now, and they're less than an hour from gaining control of those nukes."

Belarus Army/Valkyrie Base Asipovichy

Outside Asipovichy, Belarus

Jack took in everything around him as engines roared to life, hundreds of men piling into transports, a good chunk of the camp rapidly preparing to leave. His two guards escorted him to a nearby building with a sign indicating it was the brig, where he was quite certain the majority of the inmates they were expecting were drunks sleeping off a bender before being released.

They entered, Jack quickly scanning the room, finding the cages empty and a lone soldier inside who shot to his feet at the sight of whom he believed was Colonel Bogatov.

"What's the meaning of this?" the man asked, fear tinging his voice.

"Chekalov ordered him locked up until the general arrives."

The guard's eyes bulged. "Holy shit! What did you do, sir?"

Jack shrugged. "He must think I slept with his wife."

The guard laughed, as did his escorts. "I'm sure it's all a misunderstanding, sir."

"Of course it is, but I'm a team player. Colonel Chekalov has an op to run that's more important than figuring out what to do with me. I respect his decision."

The guard rounded his desk. "I'm sorry, sir, but I'll have to pat you down."

"Knock yourself out." He removed his sidearm and handed it over. The guard placed it on the corner of his desk then began his pat down, completing it within moments, finding nothing.

"If you'll follow me, sir."

Jack glanced over his shoulder at his escorts. "Thanks for taking it easy on me, boys. You could have been a lot rougher."

The escort who had done most of the talking bowed his head slightly. "One does not rough up a colonel, sir."

Jack smiled from behind the mask. "No, one doesn't." His fist darted out, crushing the man's windpipe, silencing him as Jack's foot kicked out, catching the other in the balls. He doubled over and Jack grabbed his head, twisting it violently, snapping the man's neck.

The guard manning the brig gasped and reached for his weapon. Jack grabbed his confiscated sidearm from the desk and whipped it at the man, catching him in the forehead, momentarily disorienting him as Jack put the first guard, struggling for breath, in a headlock, breaking his neck. He advanced on the final guard and the man retreated, holding up his arms, begging for mercy.

But none was to be had today.

Operations Center 3, CIA Headquarters

Langley, Virginia

"There he is."

Leroux looked up and he cocked an eyebrow in surprise. "He's not wearing his mask."

Tong turned. "Maybe because Bogatov is supposed to be locked up."

They watched as Jack slung a rifle across his back and leaped into the rear of a troop carrier as it rolled past. "Mark that truck. Make sure we've got eyes on it at all times. And let Sherrie know what vehicle he's in, just in case."

Tong turned back to her station. "Relaying now."

Child killed a spin. "I have a question."

"What?"

"Just what does Jack think he's going to do? We're counting at least a thousand troops leaving. He's just one man."

Leroux shook his head. "I don't know. But it's his job to try and stop this."

"Or die trying."

"Now that's interesting," said Tong.

"What?"

She pointed at the massive display arcing across the front of the room. "It looks like the Belarusians didn't know they were just pawns."

Leaving Belarus Army/Valkyrie Base Asipovichy

Outside Asipovichy, Belarus

Jack had always found the best way to set people at ease was with humor. Everyone in the back of the transport he had jumped into was on edge, and an unfamiliar face joining them while already underway didn't help.

"So, does anybody know if where we're going has any good whorehouses?"

The man sitting beside him grunted. "This is Belarus. I was in Minsk a couple of months ago. The prostitutes were so ugly they should have paid me."

Laughter rippled among the troops, another chiming in. "That was one of the good things about the assignment in Syria. There was always a ready supply of women willing to please for a few Euros."

"Yeah, that was a hell of a lot better assignment," agreed someone else. "Too hot, though."

"I don't know. The heat could get to you, but the mud here? My God! I'm so sick of the mud. It sticks to everything."

"I'd rather mud than dry desert sand up my crack."

More laughter.

And Jack settled in, letting the conversation continue among the friends who had trained and served together for months, if not years, his unexpected arrival forgotten, at least for the moment.

His comms squawked in his ear. "Jackrabbit, Control. We have Belarusian troops mobilizing all around your area. Washington informed them of what we think is going on, and it appears they're going to try and stop this. We recommend you abort your mission and let them deal with Valkyrie. This might be over before you can even reach the base."

He cleared his throat, a triple grunt.

Negative.

"Understood, Jackrabbit. I hope you know what you're doing."

Me too.

Gostinitsa Hotel

Asipovichy, Belarus

Sherrie groaned, having just received the latest update from Leroux. "He's still going in?"

"Yes, it would appear so."

She continued packing her bag as she prepared to leave. "I can't say I'm surprised. I'd do the same."

"You would?"

"Of course I would. Would you trust the Belarusians to be able to stop these guys? These are all battle-hardened troops, well-equipped. The Belarusians are poorly equipped, poorly trained, and lack any motivation to die for their country. Valkyrie is going to plow right through them."

Leroux sighed. "Unfortunately, that's Washington's assessment as well. They're hoping they buy enough time for Washington to discuss with our NATO allies an appropriate response should Valkyrie succeed."

Sherrie rolled her eyes. Talk, talk, talk. That's all politicians ever did. In a situation like this, action was required. Send twenty or thirty high-yield cruise missiles into the Valkyrie camp and you eliminate the problem in less than half an hour. Instead, the politicians would keep talking until the Valkyrie forces had seized the nukes, and then what did you do? "Will they respond?"

Leroux grunted. "I doubt it, though I wouldn't put it past the Poles to unilaterally act. This is on their border. And if those nukes launch, the fallout could come directly over their territory, not to mention where you are right now."

Sherrie pursed her lips. "You're right. What are my orders?"

"Assist Jack as much as possible. If those missiles launch, head back to Minsk as fast as you can and get to the embassy. They'll arrange your extraction and provide refuge from any fallout should it become necessary."

There was a pause and she waited to see what he would say.

His voice was subdued. "Bottom line, the moment you see a launch, you get the hell outta Dodge."

"What about Jack?"

"If they launch, that base will be taken out within minutes. Of that, I have no doubt."

"So, what you're saying…"

"I'm saying you save your own ass. Jack is on his own."

En Route to Yuzhny Military Base, Belarus

Jack and several of the others leaned out the back of the truck, watching as missiles streaked into the sky from behind them, one of their anti-aircraft systems engaging. An explosion in the distance indicated the defensive system had found its target, and whatever Belarusian intervention underway was, at least for the moment, failing.

He sat back down. "Looks like we won't be just walking in, boys."

Two more explosions thundered in the distance, smiles and fist bumps exchanged, the Russian-supplied state-of-the-art air defense system once again performing its magic. Unfortunately for the world, it was unlikely Valkyrie wouldn't achieve their objective despite the Belarusians' best efforts. Ironically, the only weapons system they had that could stop Valkyrie was their mission objective.

The nuclear weapons transferred to them by Russia.

Gunfire broke out ahead, a mix of AK variants rattling away. Jack readied his weapon, as did the others, the flaps on the sides of the truck pulled up as everyone turned around to face the outside. Jack peered out at the countryside with his improved view. Gunfire continued ahead, several explosions throwing debris into the air as the heavily-armed vehicles at the head of the convoy made quick work of whatever resistance the Belarusians had thrown at them.

Things were happening too fast for the defenders. Valkyrie were supposed to be their allies, their honored guests. This part of the plan hatched between the Russian president and the Valkyrie leadership had clearly been kept from their Belarusian patsies. The poor bastards didn't stand a chance. He just hoped they had time to put up a better defense at the base holding the missiles, because right now, he still had no clue how he could prevent their launch and save the lives of potentially millions.

It was simply too much to ask of any one man.

Secure Briefing Room, CIA Headquarters

Langley, Virginia

"Mr. President, it's my recommendation that we hit the Valkyrie base plus all the nuclear sites immediately. We can't risk these weapons falling into Valkyrie hands."

Morrison sat in a secure conference room, a dozen different faces on a grid on the far wall, the teleconference between the White House and several different agencies going on for far too long, everybody dancing around what needed to be done, until he had finally had enough.

The president pursed his lips, a frown creasing his face. "And what if we miss one?"

"That's always a risk, sir, but we have excellent satellite coverage. If we detect any launches, we hit them again, and we have air defense batteries all along the border. Anything they launch we can take out."

"If that's the case, then why can't we just shoot down whatever they launch at Ukraine?" asked the Secretary of Defense.

Morrison dismissed the idea and was a little pissed at the question. The man should already know the answer to this. "Because we're not in range."

"Then why can't the Ukrainians shoot them down?"

"Because we haven't supplied them with the necessary equipment. And even if we did, it might not matter."

"What do you mean?" asked the president.

"Well, sir, if I were them, I'd launch a single missile and do an air burst. That means an EMP that takes out pretty much everything electronic. The Ukrainians aren't as shielded as we are. It would collapse their communications network and they'd be defenseless against anything else incoming. Sir, if we don't act now, Kyiv could be wiped off the face of the earth before nightfall. A preemptive strike ends this."

"Leif, you're asking me to launch airstrikes against a sovereign state unprovoked, a sovereign state that has a mutual defense pact with Russia."

"I realize that, sir. However, once we take out those nukes, the Belarusians won't have anything they can hit us with, and they won't dare react."

"I don't think anybody here cares about what the Belarusians do," said the Secretary of State. "It's the Russians and how they might react."

Morrison dismissed the concern. "Mr. President, they won't do anything. Not to us. They know they can't win. Worst case scenario is that they send their forces into Belarus. They might as well already be there since the Belarusian president is a puppet of the Kremlin."

The president leaned back. "The Poles won't like that. Belarus has been a buffer between their former masters for decades now."

Morrison had to agree. "It's definitely going to change the security situation in Europe, sir, perhaps permanently, but it will save Ukraine and send a message that we won't put up with bullshit like this anymore."

The president leaned forward. "You've given us all something to think about, Leif. Keep up the good work and keep me posted. I'll let you know what we decide."

"Yes, Mr. President." The teleconference ended and Morrison cursed, turning to Leroux, who had been there in case he needed details backed up. "Well, that was a waste of time."

"You did your best, sir. It's up to them whether they listen."

Morrison regarded his young protege. "What do *you* think is going to happen? What's that famous gut of yours telling you?"

Leroux sighed. "Nothing good. If I had to hazard a guess, I'd say Valkyrie will take the base in short order. They'll launch quite possibly a single missile, like you said. And even if that's the only one they get off, the EMP will cause havoc. All their equipment that isn't shielded will be non-functional. That's cars, cellphones, TVs, radios, kitchen appliances. It'd be a disaster on an unprecedented scale. Kyiv is a city of almost three million people, and their resources are already stretched thin due to the war. If they get hit with just an EMP, the relief efforts required would be massive, and you'd be asking NGOs to enter a war zone. And it's not like any of the NATO military that would normally respond in situations like this could go in. The Russians wouldn't stand for it."

"The Russians might not have a choice."

"They might not. But what happens if a missile takes out NATO forces? Things could escalate into a full-blown war. It doesn't have to go nuclear to be a disaster. And God forbid if they launch more than one missile. Anything after the first will be a ground detonation, and each of those warheads is more powerful than the ones that destroyed Hiroshima and Nagasaki, even if they are classified today as tactical and not strategic."

"Will there be time after the first launch to stop a second?"

"It all depends. The Iskander missile systems that the Russians have supplied can launch in as little as four minutes."

Morrison cursed. "Four minutes?"

Leroux held up a finger. "Yes, but that's only if it's in a state of preparedness. Most likely they have the platforms stored, so it would take a minimum of sixteen minutes for a fully trained crew to ready the first missile for launch. But once that launch happens, depending on their setup, they could launch a second missile in as little as one minute."

Morrison's shoulders slumped. There was no way, even if NATO responded immediately after the first launch, that they could take out the Belarusian base in less than a minute. "Then it's hopeless."

Leroux shrugged. "Like I said, there are some unknown factors. It could take four minutes, it could take forty minutes, depending on how well-trained their crews are. If Valkyrie's been planning for this, then I have no doubt they have at least one crew fully trained. But I think it's fairly safe to assume the Belarusians don't have those weapons on standby. There's no need. In their minds, it was probably all for show.

They didn't realize they were pawns in a Kremlin chess game. The biggest question is the configuration, which is where we might get lucky."

Morrison cocked an eyebrow. "Oh?"

"Well, the Iskander system is capable of carrying four missiles. However, it's only capable of carrying two nukes."

"That still means one EMP detonation and another ground detonation."

"Yes, sir. However, remember I said a lot of this was for show. We have photographic evidence that the missile systems when they arrived only had one missile per platform, and a fair chunk of what we have photos of shows they were delivered with conventional weapons on the platforms themselves. It looks more impressive to see four missiles than just two or one."

Morrison held up a hand. "Wait a minute here. Are you saying there's a chance that the weapon platforms that Valkyrie's about to take over might not even have nukes on them?"

"Yes, sir. But like I said, a trained crew can be ready to launch very quickly. They would swap out the missiles and still be ready to launch. And frankly, if we're not going to do anything preemptively, they could take ten hours to ready the weapon for launch and it would make no difference."

Morrison rolled his eyes, tossing his head back in frustration. "Let's just hope that Jack can figure something out, because right now I can't see any way to avoid Ukraine getting hit with at least one nuke, if not two."

"Let's hope, sir. But frankly, I can't think of anything he can do."

En Route to Yuzhny Military Base, Belarus

Jack lay prone on the ground, the men from his transport spread out on either side, engaging a group of Belarusian soldiers hiding behind a roadblock just ahead. Mortars were being set up and the poor bastards would be taken out in short order, so he didn't have much time. As those around him fired freely, unconcerned with spending their ammo, he picked his shots, taking out the tires of several transports rather than wasting them on individual Valkyrie members.

He estimated at least a thousand were involved here. Even if he emptied all of his mags, it would barely make a dent, and he would have been killed long before he took out half a dozen. But vehicles were different. Each transport he took out meant about twenty troops would be delayed in arriving at their destination.

He had already taken out the tires of three. It would take time to change them, and since each transport only had one spare, he was taking out two tires per. The delayed Valkyrie troops would eventually get underway again, but it could make a difference in the battle to come, as the base they were heading for did have a significant number of defenders. Anything he could do to even the odds would improve the chances of those he would normally consider the enemy.

He spotted a supply truck ahead, its canvas back flapping in the wind. And he smiled. Crates of grenades. He fired several rounds into the back, not expecting an explosion, as this wasn't Hollywood and deflagration design techniques minimized the risks of unintended explosions in modern military weaponry. He was just hoping for a fire that would create panic.

The distinctive pop of mortars launching signaled the impending end to the battle, explosions tearing apart the Belarusian position. Moments later, the gunfire quickly dwindled and Valkyrie forces swarmed the roadblock, no prisoners taken. It was quickly cleared when somebody shouted, pointing toward the supply truck, smoke billowing out of the back, his shots having had their desired effect. This would definitely delay the entire column, but only for a few minutes.

But right now, minutes counted.

En Route to Yuzhny Military Base, Belarus

Sherrie peered through her binoculars, frowning as the battle unfolded, the last of the Belarusians taken out mercilessly. A piece of heavy equipment barreled through the blockade, clearing the road of the vehicles placed in the way along with the bodies of those who had given their lives to protect against the theft of the nuclear weapons.

She adjusted her gaze farther down the column. Langley had identified Jack and she checked on him for the umpteenth time. He was up on a knee, his weapon pointed ahead. He wasn't in any danger now as long as he could stay out of sight of the commanders who might recognize him. There was a scramble of activity as fire extinguishers were brought to bear on a smoking supply truck. The front of the column got underway and she smiled as Jack jumped in the back of his transport, half a dozen vehicles left behind as tires were rolled into position.

Something tells me Jack had something to do with that.

It was a help, but not much. From the looks of things, a little over a hundred men were milling about waiting for their rides to be ready, but that was only one-tenth of the force sent against the base just down the road. It wouldn't be enough. It just meant there would be reinforcements arriving five or ten minutes after the initial assault. If the Valkyrie commanders had any concern, they would merely wait for them to catch up.

At least he had tried, which was more than she had managed. Unfortunately, there was still nothing she could think of to prevent the Valkyrie attack and the inevitable taking of the base and the ultimate launching of the nukes.

It was in the hands of the politicians, and she knew how that would turn out.

Operations Center 3, CIA Headquarters

Langley, Virginia

Morrison stared in disbelief as the Valkyrie column continued its inexorable advance toward the base. He glanced over at Leroux. "Anything else standing between them and the nukes?"

Leroux pinched his chin. "Just the troops at the base."

"How many?"

"We estimate about one hundred Russian troops and about two-thousand Belarusian."

"And how many Valkyrie are they up against?"

"Almost a thousand, though whatever caused those trucks to have tire troubles has reduced that by about one-hundred-twenty, according to the computer. It helps, but not really. These guys are far better armed and trained."

"How do you think this will play out?"

Leroux waved a hand. "I suspect they'll hit the base and most of the troops there will surrender or run within the first ten minutes. Has the president made a decision yet?"

Morrison grunted. "No. He's consulting with our allies."

Child spun in his chair, growling. "Well, somebody better grow a set pretty quickly or we're up shit's creek."

Morrison chuckled. "I'll let him know you said so."

Child dropped a foot, killing his spin. "I'd rather you didn't."

"Now who needs to grow a set?" laughed Packman, reaching over and punching Child on the shoulder.

Leroux smiled as Child kicked his foot out, spinning his chair as he delivered double birds.

Morrison grinned, heading for the door. "I'm going to update the president. Even though he's well aware of what's going on, I have a funny feeling I'm the only one calling for a preemptive strike. Everyone else is advising him to keep his powder dry."

"Good luck, sir," said Leroux. "And if you think sacrificing Randy's career will help, you have my permission."

"Hey!" protested Child. "I don't consent!"

Morrison reached the door and turned toward the young man. "We may live in a democracy, but you don't work in one. If I think it can stop a war, I won't hesitate to throw you under the bus." He left a slack-jawed Child behind.

"Is he serious?"

Leroux winked at Tong. "I don't know. He sounded serious to me."

"Very serious," agreed Tong.

"I should learn to keep my mouth shut," groaned Child.

"Amen to that!" shouted Therrien from the back of the room.

But Child didn't respond in his usual manner. The poor kid was actually scared.

Leroux regarded him. "Randy."

Child looked up. "Huh?"

"He was just joking."

"What?"

"He was just joking."

Laughter erupted and Child fired a string of expletives at the room as he spun, renewed double birds accompanying the profanity. "I hate you all!"

"The feeling's mutual!" shouted Therrien.

465th Missile Brigade

Yuzhny Military Base, Belarus

Jack reloaded as he headed for the far-left flank, the assault on the main gate of the Belarusian base underway for several minutes now. Fortunately, the defenders had done something smart. They had destroyed the road and mined the main approach, forcing the Valkyrie forces to attack on foot. A flurry of projectiles from a Tornado-G multiple rocket launcher soared through the air, decimating the defenses, and Valkyrie forces surged forward. He sprinted toward the fence and pushed through a portion damaged by the strikes, then made a beeline along the front, using a building as cover from the sprinkle of defensive fire. As he had feared, those assigned to defend the base were rapidly falling back.

He rounded the other side of the building at a crouch and found a Belarusian soldier cowering in fear. He cold-cocked him, knocking him out, then took up position with a view of the gate. He left as little of himself exposed, switching to firing left-handed, and started taking single disciplined shots at the advancing Valkyrie forces, each round finding their mark.

"Two Russian hostiles coming down the fence line behind you," reported Tong in his ear. "Twenty seconds."

"Copy that." He fell back and turned, taking both out as they came around the corner. He could have used them in the battle, but it was too risky to try and convince them he was on their side. They were the enemy. In fact, everyone here was his enemy. How the hell was he supposed to deal with over 3,000 hostiles by himself? This was ridiculous. Somebody somewhere had to grow some balls. An air-strike could take out the nukes in minutes, but NATO's political leaders refused to act.

Cowards.

Sherrie sprinted toward the battle, having gotten as close as she dared in her SUV in the bright daylight. The battle had been raging for about ten minutes, Valkyrie forces spread out across the front of the base, pouring heavy fire on the defenders. Her briefing had the missiles located in the rear half of the base to the right of her current position, and it appeared Valkyrie was carefully avoiding hitting that area.

There was no risk of a nuclear detonation due to a stray shot—nukes didn't work that way, but if they destroyed the launch platforms, they wouldn't be able to use the weapons they had come to capture. Langley, still in her ear, had reported that Jack was spotted penetrating the fence and was now inside the base. She still had no clue what he hoped to accomplish, nor did she know what she could possibly accomplish, though like him, she had to try something.

They had no choice.

She reached the rear of the massive convoy and found no one nearby, the troop transports near the rear empty, the personnel they carried either at or heading for the battle. She planted a small explosive near the gas tank of the rear transport, then advanced to the next, finding it empty as well. She continued forward, planting several more explosives every third vehicle, counting on secondary detonations to take out those in between.

She had planted half a dozen of the devices before she heard voices ahead. She darted off the road and into the weeds, pausing and listening for any indication she had been detected, but heard nothing beyond the continuing battle. She headed farther from the road and into the tall wheat stalks planted by a local farmer, the grain high enough to provide good cover.

She pulled out her phone and set off the bombs, the small explosives tearing at the trucks, fuel spilling onto the ground from the ruptured tanks, the flames from the detonations igniting the fuel. Half a dozen large fires quickly raged, engulfing the other vehicles in short order.

Shouts erupted as the flame spread and she took the opportunity to rush ahead while Valkyrie forces raced to the rear of the convoy to see what had happened. More explosions sent them scrambling from the road as the fire spread forward. The vehicles were packed so tightly together, two and three abreast, those loaded with combustible supplies helping add to the mass confusion now breaking out. The Valkyrie rushing to investigate hugged the ground, desperate to avoid the detonations as fuel and ammo exploded.

She kept her head down and sprinted as fast as she could, tossing more of the magnetic charges toward the convoy, flicking their detonators to activate five seconds after contact before throwing them. Trucks blasted apart as she continued when Leroux's voice delivered a warning.

"Hit the dirt!"

She dropped, not questioning the voice in her ear. Bullets chewed up the air overhead as someone opened up on the wheat fields. "Where do I go?"

"Keep heading forward. It's what they'd least expect."

US V Corps Headquarters (Forward)

Camp Kościuszko, Poland

The overhead PA system squawked an urgent announcement in Polish. Spock cocked an eyebrow at the speaker. "Does anybody know any Polish?"

Jimmy shrugged. "Do my dad's Polish jokes count?"

Spock gave him a look. "Something tells me, no."

Dawson's comms beeped. "Bravo Zero-One, this is Control Actual. Come in, over."

"Go ahead, Control."

"Your status has been changed. Operation Jack Out of The Box is a go."

Dawson rose as did the others. "Acknowledged, Control, heading for our ride now. What's the overall situation? Our Polish hosts seem pretty excited about something." More announcements blared and boots pounded on the floor outside their door, all of it suggesting nothing routine.

"Valkyrie forces are attacking Yuzhny Military Base where some of the nukes are being held. It looks like they're going to have control shortly. NATO has issued warnings to Moscow, Minsk, and Valkyrie that any launch will be met with overwhelming force."

Dawson grunted as they filed out into the corridor, already geared up. "Any response?"

"What do you think?"

Dawson chuckled at Leroux's reply. "Yeah, I didn't think so. And do we actually think NATO is going to respond?" he asked as they jogged down the corridor, everyone getting out of their way, for even though they were the guests here, geared up, they were as intimidating as hell.

"That's the question, isn't it? All I can tell you is that all across NATO, anything within reach of Belarus has gone on alert."

A sound Dawson recognized interrupted Leroux's end of the conversation and they both cursed.

"Is that what I think it is?"

Leroux confirmed his worst fears. "Yes. We've just gone to DEFCON Three."

465th Missile Brigade

Yuzhny Military Base, Belarus

Jack poured lead on those advancing then fell back, rounding the building as Belarusian and Russian defenders regrouped, putting up a stiffer resistance than in the earlier minutes of this battle. But it was a hopeless cause. There were over one thousand well-equipped, well-trained men with the element of relative surprise. No one at this base had ever expected to be attacked. Ukraine was far enough away that it was never a real threat, and NATO would never attack first. The battle was likely hopeless, yet every man he took out helped, albeit if only a little.

Sherrie had arrived, the latest update from Langley in his ear indicating she was wreaking havoc at the far end of the column, troop carriers and supply trucks aflame. Though that would result in minimal, if any casualties, it would be enough to hopefully cause some of the Valkyrie forces to fall back and guard their rear. If it took fifty to one hundred men out of the mix, even if only for a few minutes, it could take some of the pressure off the defenders, giving them a chance to regroup.

"Take cover! Incoming!"

Leroux's warning had him dropping and rolling under a building as a heavy barrage of rockets streaked overhead, hammering the base, the ground shuddering with each impact.

"Report!"

"They're hitting most of the base hard. We recommend you move toward the number one side. The closer you get to the Valkyrie forces, the less chance of you getting hit."

"Copy that." Jack rolled back out and pushed to his feet, making for the fence line at the front of the base.

"The Belarusians are falling back."

He cursed. "And the Russians?"

"They're consolidating around the nukes."

"Copy that." He continued forward, the fence line in sight, when a burst of static filled his ear. He frowned and rounded the corner blind, only to run headlong into Chekalov.

"What the hell are you doing here?"

Operations Center 3, CIA Headquarters

Langley, Virginia

Leroux tapped his headset then turned to Tong. "Are they jamming us?"

Tong worked her station then threw up her hands. "I'm not picking him up anymore."

"Check Sherrie's comms."

More frustration. "Negative. She's not responding either."

Leroux cursed. "They must have activated some sort of jammer."

Child's eyes narrowed. "Won't that kill their comms as well?"

"Yes, but they've planned for this. They just need to execute their mission. Once the defenders realize they can't reach any of their commanders, they're going to abandon their posts." Leroux pointed at the satellite feed. "Look, it's already starting." He watched as scores of defenders streamed out the back gate.

Packman frowned. "I guess we know why they only hit the front. They wanted to give everyone a way out."

Leroux frowned as Valkyrie forces surged forward, pressing their advantage. This battle was lost. "Do we have an angle on Jack?"

"Negative. The satellite's too low in the sky. Last we had was him rounding a building at the one-two corner," reported Tong. "Let me look for a better view." She cycled through the various satellite feeds, finally settling on one. She cursed. "I found him."

"And so did they," muttered Child.

465th Missile Brigade

Yuzhny Military Base, Belarus

Jack's rifle butt darted upward but Chekalov easily defended against the move, shoving it aside. He was well trained, combat-hardened in not only the Ukrainian campaign but with Spetsnaz. Jack had read all the files on the senior commanders they had managed to identify, Sherrie having provided the files last night. He wasn't winning this fight. While he might defeat Chekalov, the twenty other guys who had their colonel's back would be more than he could handle.

But he might as well have some fun with it.

He tossed his weapon aside then threw a punch that was parried, a counterpunch delivered. Jack ducked, avoiding it, snapping out a kick that was blocked. A rapid series of fists and feet were thrown, few blows landing, as Valkyrie troops surrounded them in a circle, eliminating any hopes he might have of escaping.

Chekalov stopped, holding out his hands in front of him. "This is getting us nowhere. Your choice. What do you wanna do?"

Jack took in the scores of guns pointed at him, then pointed at Chekalov. "I'll give you one chance to surrender."

Chekalov and the others laughed. "You've got a good sense of humor. It's too bad you're going to die."

Jack shrugged. "Kill me now, please. That way I can't tell you who among you is the traitor."

"Nice try. You're the traitor."

Jack smirked. "Oh, I am all right, but I don't work alone. And ask yourself this, why did the general let me run the mission to Moscow, and where is he now?"

This caught Chekalov off guard, his eyes narrowing. "What are you saying?"

Jack shrugged. "I'm not saying anything, but if I were you, I'd be having serious second thoughts about your mission. Right now, you're the ones who will be blamed and left hung out to dry."

"What do you know of the mission? There are only a handful of people here that know it, and two in Moscow. How could you possibly know?"

Jack chuckled. "Remember, I'm not working alone."

Sherrie whipped one of her few remaining magnetic explosives at the mobile jammer, the puck attaching to the side of the truck detonating several seconds later, the rear compartment tearing apart. The static in her ear instantly cleared and she continued forward at a crouch, the wheat stalks still covering her position. "Control, Skylark, do you read?"

She could almost hear the relief in Leroux's voice. "We've got you, Skylark. Status?"

"I just took out the jammer. We should be good for comms. Status on Jackrabbit?"

"He's in custody. They're taking him deeper into the base, likely toward the nukes."

A frown creased her face as she approached the fence line. "At least they haven't killed him yet. I need a path in if I'm going to rescue him."

"Negative, Skylark. There are too many of them. We recommend you begin your withdrawal to Minsk."

She rolled her eyes at the suggestion. "Not going to happen, Control. Now, are you gonna help me, or am I doing this on my own?"

She could hear the frustration in her boyfriend's voice, though he shouldn't have been surprised by her answer. It was the same answer any operative would give. "Fine. Pull back from the road to avoid the search parties. We'll let you know where they take Jack. And try not to get yourself killed."

"Aw, you still love me despite me not following your recommendation?"

"No, I just hate the paperwork involved."

"Cheeky. You'll be paying for that one when I get back."

"Can't wait if it means getting you back alive."

She laughed.

God, I love that man.

Heavy gunfire rattled ahead, AK-47s and 74s exchanging fire, both sides in this battle equipped by the same source. Mother Russia. On their private assignments, Valkyrie mercenaries quite often had their own weapons of choice, but here in the midst of the war with Ukraine, they used the same weaponry the Russian Army did, which meant fewer supply issues. It made it difficult to determine just who was winning this battle, though he had little doubt it was Valkyrie.

Chekalov led his men forward toward the fighting. Jack was flanked by four guards, his arms gripped by two of them as he sought any means of escape, though perhaps escape wasn't the correct course of action here. He was being led toward the fighting, and the fighting, according to the last update from Langley, was surrounding the building that contained the nukes.

He had the impression Chekalov didn't want to let him out of his sight, and if he was in command of this operation, then Jack might be led straight to the nukes. What the hell he would do when he was within sight of them, he wasn't sure. He could probably take out his four guards with little problem.

It was the other 1004 that might prove more challenging.

Chekalov pointed toward a gap between two buildings. "Hold him there. If he tries anything, shoot him. I have to deal with these Russians."

"Yes, sir," said one of the guards, and Jack was led away while Chekalov and the others rushed forward, their guns joining the fray a moment later, leaving Jack with a decision.

Kill the guards, or just wait to be invited in?

An explosion from behind them had everyone turning, black smoke billowing into the sky. A moment later Jack's comms, buried deep in his ear canal and missed during the pat-down, squawked, the jammer obviously having been taken out in the explosion he had just heard.

Way to go, Sherrie!

"Jackrabbit, Control Actual. We just got comms back thanks to Skylark. We've got you on satellite. We're going to monitor your situation then Skylark will attempt a rescue."

He cleared his throat.

Negative.

"I've already told her to fall back to Minsk, but she refuses, so expect an attempt. The Belarusians have abandoned their positions and are retreating en masse through the rear gate. The Russians are defending the storage facility where the missiles are located. Intel indicates there are six Iskander mobile missile systems located inside. They have to be prepped before launch. A trained crew takes a minimum of sixteen minutes, so once they take the facility, if we're lucky, we've got maybe twenty minutes to prevent this. Unfortunately, at this time, don't expect a response from NATO. If there's any hope of stopping this, it's up to you."

A cough.

Understood.

The gunfire ahead dwindled, signaling his twenty-minute deadline was about to begin. He glanced at his escorts. "Looks like you guys are going to win the day."

One of them smirked. "Was there ever any doubt?"

"No. General Pikalov and I both agreed we would have no trouble getting this far."

The man eyed him. "Bullshit. You were a stray, picked up a few days ago on a bridge in Ukraine. I was there."

"Yes, you were. And did you ever ask yourself how I gained the trust of the general so quickly, and why he had me pose as Colonel Bogatov after he was murdered by someone in our camp?"

The man's eyes narrowed. "Wait, Colonel Bogatov is dead?"

"Yes, since before we left Ukraine. I have been wearing his mask and ring for days now. General Pikalov knows exactly who I am. My rescue was staged to get me inside."

"Why would he need to do that? Why not just bring you in?"

"Because he wanted someone from the outside to help root out the traitor."

"And did you?" asked one of the others.

"Yes. It was Colonel Bogatov."

All four men recoiled in horror at the lie.

"I don't believe you."

Jack shrugged. "Doesn't matter. He's dead. I'm here and General Pikalov wants me here. Kill me and you're dead. Don't stop this"—he twirled his finger in the air at the goings-on—"and we're all dead before nightfall."

One of them laughed. "There's no way they can stop us."

Jack regarded the man. "Do you even know what's going on here?"

"I don't need to know. I just follow orders."

"Then let me explain. We're here to launch the nukes that are stored in the building not one hundred meters from where we stand. Within an hour, Kyiv will be destroyed, hundreds of thousands will be dead, and NATO *will* respond. This base will be destroyed, as will our shiny new base where the rest of our brothers are, and the world will be on the brink of World War Three."

The gunfire ahead stopped and Jack jerked his chin toward the front line. "Looks like you're going to have a decision to make, boys. That silence means the nukes are ours and the blood they shed is on your hands. Ask yourselves this. Can you live with the knowledge you could have done something to prevent the deaths of potentially millions, but instead stood by for a payday that will never come? When you answer to God for your sins, will He accept the excuse that you were just following orders and it wasn't your fault?"

His lead escort's radio squawked. "Bring the traitor."

The man raised his radio to his lips. "On our way, sir."

Jack regarded him then the others. "Last chance, boys."

He was grabbed by both arms once again and shoved forward. "You're a spy. I don't believe a word you're saying."

Jack shrugged. "Then I guess we all die."

Sherrie inched forward along the number two side of the base, left of the main gate. The gunfire was sporadic now, the battle for the nukes having been lost by what she hesitated to call the good guys. That meant in as little as sixteen minutes there could be a launch, and so far, NATO had shown no sign they were going to do anything about it beyond rattle their limp sabers.

"You've got a group of Russians ahead of you hiding in the hedgerow," reported Leroux.

"How many?" she whispered.

"Three."

"Copy that. I'm going to try something."

She headed toward the Russians, the panic in their harsh whispers evident.

"What do we do?"

"What can we do? There's too many of them."

"But if they get control of those nukes—"

She finished the thought for them. "Then we're responsible for the deaths of potentially millions."

All three spun toward her, reaching for their weapons. She held up her empty hands. "Special Agent Nadia Abisov, FSB. I'm here to help."

A sergeant eyed her. "What's one woman going to do?"

"More than any of you have so far, apparently. I've taken out at least a dozen of their vehicles, including their jammer. My partner is inside the base, and he's taken out dozens. But you're right, it isn't enough. We need to regroup for a counterattack."

This had three sets of eyes bulging as if they all thought she was insane.

"Those missiles can't be allowed to fall into enemy hands. They intend to launch them against Ukraine and destroy Kyiv."

"But that's mass murder!" exclaimed a private.

"Yes, it is. But they're Valkyrie. Do you think they give a shit about such things? And do you think the world will care it was Valkyrie that launched and not Mother Russia? We will be blamed, like we always are. If you think things are hard for our countrymen now, just wait until we're blamed for killing hundreds of thousands, perhaps millions. Our country will be isolated and destroyed economically. Even the Chinese won't have anything to do with us." She pointed toward the battle. "We need to stop this before it's too late. Are you with me?"

Heads bobbed, though reluctantly.

"Good. Let's gather some allies because you're right. Four of us aren't enough."

Operations Center 3, CIA Headquarters

Langley, Virginia

Leroux tossed his head back, pulling at his hair. "She's insane!"

"She is that," agreed Morrison. "But she's good."

Leroux let out an exasperated sigh. "Too good for her own good."

Morrison laughed. "True. But one day, she'll be up there in the ranks, like Kane and Jack. She has the potential to become a legend."

Leroux frowned. "If she doesn't get herself killed first."

"Agreed. So, let's do whatever we can to make sure that doesn't happen."

Leroux threw a hand toward the tactical display, showing no movement west of the Belarusian border. "Is NATO ever going to respond?"

"They're still holding for evidence that the missiles are actually going to be launched. The Ukrainians are begging for them to launch a preemptive strike now, but the NATO leaders are agreed that they can't make the first move."

Child spun in his chair, a growl erupting. "First move? What the hell do they call this? If this isn't a first move, I don't know what is."

Morrison regarded the young man. "I agree, and have said that repeatedly. But everyone is terrified of hitting a nuclear weapons facility with Russian soldiers manning it."

"So, let's just sacrifice Kyiv then respond? If that's not the most cowardly chicken shit political decision I've ever heard of—"

Morrison cut him off. "You're preaching to the choir, son. Let's just hope Jack and Sherrie can do something before it's too late."

Leroux sighed. "Jack's in custody and Sherrie only has three Russians that already ran away once. What the hell can they do?"

465th Missile Brigade

Yuzhny Military Base, Belarus

Jack was led inside the massive hangar and he frowned at the sight of half a dozen 9K720 Iskander mobile short-range ballistic missile systems, all lined up neatly, emergency lighting casting sinister shadows around them. The power had been cut off by the Belarusians as he was led inside, but no one here appeared concerned. And why should they? The fact they had gotten this far with no response from NATO showed the military organization controlled by political masters was wrought with indecision, as he had expected.

Goodbye, Ukraine, it was nice knowing you.

Look out, Taiwan, China's coming for you.

The world was about to fall apart, the Western democracies that were supposed to be the future, crumbling with infighting, where countries split along political lines hated their opponents more than they loved their country. It was disgusting, and part of him wanted to just sit back and let it all burn, let humanity destroy itself, and a thousand years from now, perhaps civilization would reemerge from the ashes as it had after the Dark Ages, and build a better society free of the hatred consuming this one.

If the streets of Western democracies were now filled with millions demanding mass murder, had these beacons of democracy already failed? Was the toothpaste already out of the tube with no hope of putting it back in? How do you reverse the damage already done?

He feared it was already too late. Even if peace came to the Middle East, it would be temporary, and those supporting the violence back home had already revealed their true colors. Yet could we blame them when half of America hated the other half with equal zeal? Were we any better? Was the West really any better than what used to be called the East? He wasn't so sure anymore.

Chekalov approached and Jack regarded him. "Congratulations on your victory. When do you start Armageddon?"

Chekalov chuckled. "A typical overreaction from doves like yourself. It's time the hawks ruled, and this will ensure it. We will be victorious in Ukraine. We will then press our advantage and reunite all Russian-speaking people and all former Soviet territories under one banner."

"The Swastika?"

Chekalov stared at him. "Don't try to provoke me. It won't work."

Jack shrugged. "It was worth a try. Perhaps a nice red flag with a smiling picture of your glorious president in the center rather than Lenin."

"Perhaps. But we will be strong once again and the West will tremble at our might."

"I doubt that. If anything, we'll be even more resolved in our fight against you, so much so you'll be left isolated, impoverished, and starving." He turned to his escort. "See, I told you what was going on. Now do you believe me?"

The sergeant stepped forward. "Is this true? Are you going to launch these nukes?"

Chekalov glared at him. "It's none of your concern." He pointed at Jack. "You just watch him. Shoot him if he even opens his mouth."

"Yes, sir," replied the sergeant, though it was clear to Jack the man wasn't pleased.

The hangar doors rolled open, manpower rather than motors shoving them aside as half a dozen Valkyrie personnel rushed in, surrounding the first weapon system.

And beginning the countdown.

Sixteen minutes to launch.

What the hell am I going to do?

Sherrie kneeled at the center of a cluster of thirty Russian and Belarusian troops they had managed to gather, and so far no one had questioned her identity or authority. They just took the word of the original three she had encountered that she was FSB, and that was enough for even the officers here, though there wasn't anyone beyond a captain.

"There's not enough of us to take back the base," said the captain. "There must be almost a thousand troops."

She nodded. "I agree. Our only hope at the moment is to cause panic in the ranks. You all have your rifles and you all have ammo. I want you to spread out around the base in pairs, but leave the main gate clear. We want them to have a route to escape." She tapped her watch. "In exactly five minutes, you'll begin taking out single targets, then repositioning and repeating the process every sixty seconds. That means fifteen teams taking out one target per minute. It means we can take out well over a hundred of them before they've had a chance to prep the first missile for launch. Are you ready?"

"Yes, ma'am!" the men echoed.

"Then let's go kill some Valkyrie pieces of shit, and save our country."

Operations Center 3, CIA Headquarters

Langley, Virginia

Morrison and Leroux stood staring at the display, the overhead satellite shot showing the cluster of ragtag defenders pulled together by Sherrie splitting up in twos and spreading around the base.

Morrison shook his head. "I can't believe an American woman is leading Russian and Belarusian troops against Russian Valkyrie mercenaries."

Leroux pinched the bridge of his nose, closing his eyes, his heart racing, his stomach churning, but his emotions, for the moment, under control. "If they only knew."

"If only." Morrison regarded him. "Well, I hate to say it, Chris, but if she survives this, it'll be a miracle, and if she does and succeeds, it'll be something historians will never write about. Not because it'll be classified, but because nobody would believe it." He turned to the room. "We could be witnessing history here, people." He pointed at the screen.

"That woman is as brave as any operative I have ever commanded. Pray for her, if you believe in such things. She's going to need it."

Leroux closed his eyes once again, saying a silent prayer for the only woman he had ever loved, and one for the Russian and Belarusian troops she was with, something he could never have dreamed of doing even just an hour ago.

Praying for the success of his enemy over a greater enemy.

The enemy of my enemy is my friend?

Well, he wouldn't go that far.

465th Missile Brigade

Yuzhny Military Base, Belarus

Jack watched as the first weapons platform continued to be prepared, Chekalov coordinating, a small black book in his hand as he worked the control panel on the launcher. Jack's 20/20 vision had picked out handwriting, not typed text. It wasn't some sort of manual, it was a notebook. It had to contain the launch codes. If he could get his hands on that book and destroy it, he might stop the remaining missiles from being launched, though it would appear the first was going to take flight unless NATO reacted.

But that wasn't going to happen. NATO wasn't a first-strike organization, and you had to wonder if they would react at all. After all, it was Ukraine being targeted. They weren't a NATO member. They weren't covered by Article 5 where an attack on one was an attack on all. Would they consider the fallout an attack if it drifted to the West? He doubted it. They had to forget Article 5. It didn't apply in this case, but morality still did. Responding was the right thing to do. Preventing this catastrophe was even more right.

Langley was well aware of what was going on, that Valkyrie had taken the missiles, and with his comms still active, they were hearing everything going on around him. That meant Washington knew, that meant NATO knew, as did all the leaders of Europe.

Yet there was still no reaction.

His four guards were in a huddle nearby, a discussion underway that from the tone and the odd word he could pick up, suggested they weren't happy about what was going on. It was interesting, if he thought about it. There were very few Valkyrie personnel inside the hangar. He counted twelve plus his four guards, and they were only here because of him. He had sowed enough doubt with Chekalov that he hadn't been summarily executed. That decision was being left for Pikalov, but it likely meant that the nearly thousand troops outside this hangar had no idea what was actually going on.

Certainly, his escorts had had no clue.

Gunfire rang out from beyond the walls, a series of single shots, then silence.

"What the hell was that?" exclaimed Chekalov.

Jack shrugged. "I don't know, but I'm guessing somebody's fighting back. You haven't won the day yet."

Sherrie scrambled twenty yards to her left, counting off sixty seconds in her head. She lay back down, prone, picking a target, Valkyrie forces pouring toward the fence line to check on their downed brothers and see what was going on. Few took cover, either ignorant of the danger, or convinced they had already won the battle.

Cocky.

Three, two, one…

She fired, shots all around her following, more of the enemy dropping as she once again scurried through the farmer's field, once again counting down from sixty, and smiled as shouts began from within the captured base, sounds of panic and confusion.

Exactly what she wanted.

Jack had estimated that between the two separate volleys, it had been approximately one minute. It had begun a countdown, and when the next volley occurred, almost exactly sixty seconds later, he suppressed the urge to smile at the disciplined counterattack underway. His trained ear suggested at least a dozen weapons involved, the limited number indicating why this method of counterattack was being used.

They didn't have enough personnel for an all-out assault.

This was merely an antagonization mission. It was meant to keep Valkyrie off their game, to sow panic among the ranks. It had to be Sherrie. CIA operations officers were trained in guerrilla warfare techniques, and if he had to hazard a guess, she had the base surrounded with about a dozen fire teams, each taking single shots at one-minute intervals, then repositioning.

If they were decent shots, ten or more of the enemy could be taken out of the equation every minute, and that quickly added up, especially when they began to fall back and take cover, abandoning their positions.

The question was, would they completely abandon their posts and leave?

Operations Center 3, CIA Headquarters

Langley, Virginia

Tong pointed at the screen. "We've got more troops joining in."

Leroux stared as troops from around the base returned in small groups, curious as to what was going on, then joining in, some setting up supply lines to make sure those already in position didn't run out of ammo. Five more fire teams had joined the original fifteen, and so far, Valkyrie hadn't managed to take a single counter-attacker out, including Sherrie.

Confusion had set in.

Pikalov wasn't there, Bogatov was dead, and Chekalov was in the hangar along with several other commanders from what had been overheard via Jack's live comms. The men outside were leaderless and uncertain as to what to do, and Sherrie's troops continued to fire every minute like clockwork, something Valkyrie had finally figured out after ten minutes, most rushing for cover just ahead of the next volley.

But not all of them.

There were always stragglers, always those too curious for their own good, always those who hadn't got the word, and ten to twenty dropped, dead or wounded, every minute.

"Do we have an estimate?" asked Morrison.

Tong nodded. "The computer's counting. At least one-hundred-and-fifty-two casualties after that last round."

Leroux pointed. "They're starting to fall back toward their vehicles."

Morrison's head bobbed in satisfaction. "Good. If Sherrie can just keep them together, then we might just stop this yet."

Leroux glanced at the timer, well past the sixteen-minute mark, not sharing his boss' optimism.

The battle to prevent the first nuke from launching was already lost.

465th Missile Brigade

Yuzhny Military Base, Belarus

Jack watched as the Valkyrie crew continued to prep the first of the mobile launchers. Chekalov stood at the control panel, the launch instructions contained in a metal-clad binder attached next to it. The man flipped through each laminated page, calling out the checklist, his crew responding. A trained crew could prep the system in sixteen minutes, and it appeared these men knew what they were doing. They could have been training for days, weeks, or even months for this operation. And it was quite possible some of these men might have trained for years on this very system when they were members of the Russian Army.

According to the time count Langley was giving him in his ear, fifteen minutes had passed several minutes ago, but these men were being careful, double and triple checking everything. It was clear they wanted nothing to go wrong, and he was of mixed feelings on the matter, though he supposed he wasn't. If something were to go wrong and the missile was to detonate here, vaporizing them all including himself, he would be fine with that if it meant saving the lives of hundreds of thousands, perhaps millions, of innocents.

He would earn his star on the wall at CIA headquarters, and deservedly so. As would Sherrie, whose counterattack was apparently reaping dividends. He liked her. She was his kind of people, and a hell of a partner even though he was accustomed to working alone. It would be a shame for someone so young to die, but if she did, saving countless lives, he just hoped the history books would record her involvement rather than leaving her unnamed like the telling of these events so often did.

Chekalov stepped back from the control panel. "System shows ready. Report any concerns."

Each of the crew prepping the system stepped back, reporting one at a time. "No concerns, sir!"

Chekalov pointed at one of the men. "Get her out to the launch site."

"Yes, sir."

The man climbed into the cab and the engine roared to life. Jack muttered a curse, his eyes darting about, helplessly searching for something he could do but coming up empty yet again. Gears ground as the driver struggled to put the massive piece of machinery into gear. He finally managed and popped the clutch, the mobile missile platform jerking forward, slowly pulling through the hangar doors and out of sight, the gears changing several more times as it was moved to the launch site.

Chekalov pointed at the next launcher. "Let's get going. I want to be launching a second missile in sixteen minutes."

"Yes, sir!"

The men went to work and Chekalov strode over to Jack. "Anything smart to say now, asshole?"

Jack eyed him, deadpan. "You haven't succeeded yet."

Chekalov smirked. "And neither have you or the mighty NATO Alliance."

Sherrie squeezed the trigger and another Valkyrie mercenary dropped as she rolled several times to her left before pushing to her knees and sprinting away. The volley of gunshots, all seemingly waiting on her initial shot, echoed around her, the sounds of more panic from the base and their enemy, almost heartwarming. She dove to the ground, quickly finding her next target, the mental count continuing in her head as an engine roared to life at the head of the convoy. She glanced over and caught sight of a light-armored vehicle turning around, its tires spinning as the driver gunned them into the farmer's field then turned, heading parallel to the road jam-packed with Valkyrie equipment.

Three, two, one…

She pulled the trigger again, taking out yet another Valkyrie piece of shit as he sprinted toward the convoy. She rolled again as someone opened fire on her former position. Valkyrie was organizing, and her teams would start taking casualties if they weren't already, but more were joining, according to Langley. They were up to thirty teams of two, spread around the base, leaving the front side free so Valkyrie had an escape route.

Her comms beeped. "Skylark, Control Actual. You lost two teams that time. Valkyrie is wise to what's going on."

"Understood, Control. I'm amazed it worked for so long. Body count?"

"Over two hundred dead or wounded."

Another engine revved hard.

"A second vehicle is leaving. Looks like about ten hostiles have left with more falling back toward the convoy. I think you're about to reach a tipping point. They seem to be taking advantage of the schedule you're on."

"That was the point. If they know they're safe for a minute at a time, every time, they can use that to retreat."

Leroux made a suggestion that he had to know she would reject. "Maybe you should hold back before they take you out."

"Negative. Until I see a wholesale retreat, we keep firing."

An alarm sounded. It wasn't a base-wide alarm. It was highly localized, just ahead. She peered through the weeds between the crops and the fence line, and cursed at the sight of a missile rising above the rooftops as its launcher prepared to deliver death and destruction upon the innocent.

"Is that what I think it is?"

"Yes. They're about to launch the first nuke."

Her shoulders slumped. "Then we failed."

An alarm sounded and Jack cursed as he recognized it as the missile launcher warning anyone in the vicinity to get clear. Chekalov smirked then turned toward the open hangar doors, and Jack made a Hail Mary attempt at stopping this once and for all. His hand darted out and he grabbed Chekalov by the throat, squeezing hard, digging his nails in and yanking back with full force, tearing the man's throat out.

Chekalov's eyes bulged as he dropped to his knees, clutching at his neck. Shouts erupted from the crew arming the next system and weapons swung toward him. Gunshots echoed in the confines of the hangar as he dropped, grabbing the still-dying Chekalov and using him as a human shield. Assault rifles opened up behind him from his guards and he cringed. But they weren't aimed at him. They were directed at the other Valkyrie forces, most of them caught by surprise. A flurry of gunfire in both directions lasted only seconds before the weapons fell silent. He peered out from behind Chekalov to see the Valkyrie crew all dead, then glanced over his shoulder to find only one of his guards still alive, though wounded.

He shoved Chekalov to the ground and smiled at him. "I told you it wasn't over till it's over."

As if to make a liar of him, a low rumble shook the hangar, the sound growing in intensity, the shaking of the ground causing him to stumble as flame and debris sprayed through the open doors to his right, signaling the launch of the deadly nuclear missile.

Chekalov grabbed him and pulled him closer, sneering at him. "We win."

Operations Center 3, CIA Headquarters

Langley, Virginia

"Oh my god!" cried Tong as Leroux shot to his feet, the entire operations center in shock at the sight of the massive plume erupting from the bottom of the missile as it thrust into the sky.

Morrison grabbed the nearest phone, rapidly dialing a number. "This is Morrison. We have a confirmed launch! I repeat, we have a confirmed launch!" He snapped his fingers. "Target?"

Leroux worked his station, bringing up the computer's projection. "Too soon to tell, but it's on a trajectory for Kyiv, as we predicted."

Morrison put the mouthpiece back in position. "It looks like Kyiv…Yes, sir, I'll let them know…Yes, Mr. President. God help us all." He hung up and Leroux stared at the man.

"Well?"

Morrison sighed. "Once again, we're late to the party."

Tong pointed at the display. "The Ukrainians are launching."

"Are they in range?" asked Morrison.

"What they're launching is, but they don't have a lot of long-range weaponry. We haven't provided them with much because we didn't want them hitting Russian territory."

Child spun in his chair. "Sometimes I think we're led by idiots."

Morrison glanced back at him. "That's been true throughout time."

Tong pointed again. "The Poles are launching."

"Good. It looks like they're taking the lead on the counterstrike."

"Cruise missiles are being launched from the Baltic Sea and land bases in Poland, Germany, Romania, Hungary, and Czech. It looks like the Belarusian army is about to be wiped off the face of the earth, as well as Valkyrie's new base and the other nuke sites. From what I can tell, they're the primary targets and will be hit first."

"Send Delta in." Leroux fit his headset in place. "We have to tell Jack and Sherrie to get the hell out of Dodge if they can. The ground they're standing on is about to be rearranged."

En Route to Yuzhny Military Base, Belarus

Niner leaned forward, his voice raised over the thundering rotors overhead. "So, let me get this straight. We're going up against Belarusian forces, Russian forces, and Valkyrie forces, and the only people on our side are Jack and Sherrie?"

Dawson nodded. "That about sums it up."

"Yeah, those seem like reasonable odds."

Atlas grunted. "At least this time our ROEs allow us to shoot first, ask questions later."

Niner grinned. "I do like that. It's so refreshing. Normally, we have to let them fire the RPG at us before we can respond."

"There's a difference this time," said Jimmy.

Spock cocked an eyebrow. "What's that?"

"If this thing goes south, the bastards who set those ROEs are within reach of the nukes that could be flying if we fail."

Niner stabbed a finger at Jimmy. "That's exactly right! The restrictions of our ROEs are inversely proportional to the risk that those who set them are in. I didn't realize that until just now."

"Consider yourself educated."

Dawson's comms demanded his attention and he raised a finger, silencing his men.

"Zero-One, Control Actual. Come in, over."

"Go ahead, Control."

"Status update. We have confirmed launch of a nuke."

A wave of nausea washed through Dawson, his face paling. "ETA to detonation?"

Shock registered throughout the helicopter, even among the crew.

"Pentagon estimates approximately five minutes."

Dawson held up his hand, displaying five fingers. "Acknowledged, Control. What are our orders?"

"You've been cleared to cross the border and attempt extraction of our assets."

"Permission to engage Valkyrie forces upon our arrival? Maybe we can stop them from any further launches."

"Negative, Zero-One, that's not the mission. Extract our assets. You'll likely see evidence of NATO's response any moment now."

"Any chance Jack might be able to stop this?"

"Negative. As far as we can tell, he's still in Valkyrie custody."

A familiar klaxon rang in the background and Dawson closed his eyes.

"Zero-One, we've just gone to DEFCON Two."

"Understood. Zero-One, out."

"What the hell's going on?" asked Niner, any hint of his usual jovial self gone.

"Valkyrie launched a nuke. Pentagon thinks it'll reach its target in five minutes."

Atlas cursed. "And that was a minute ago. What the hell happens now?"

Dawson clenched his fists in frustration. "We execute our mission. Unfortunately, by the time we get there, this will either all be over, or we could be in a full-fledged war."

Coincidence lit up the horizon as NATO responded, dozens of targets erupting in balls of flame ahead as their pilot, who had received his own separate orders, announced they had crossed the border.

Bravo Team would be the first NATO soldiers to engage the enemy in the feared expansion of the Ukraine-Russia war.

God help us all.

465th Missile Brigade

Yuzhny Military Base, Belarus

Jack grabbed the guard's hand and pressed it over the man's wound. "You good?"

"No." The young man reached up and grabbed him by the collar. "Tell my mother I'm sorry. Tell her I did the right thing in the end."

Jack squeezed the young man's shoulder. "I will, kid. You can count on it."

The man collapsed, his chest still. Jack removed the dead man's wallet so he could identify him later and keep his promise. He shoved it in his pocket then grabbed the black book from Chekalov. He retrieved a sidearm and an AK-47, along with several mags, off the body of one of his dead guards, then flipped through the pages of the notebook.

"Jackrabbit, Control Actual. Come in, over."

Jack headed for the doors. "Go ahead, Control." Gunfire continued outside, Sherrie's assault wreaking havoc. Valkyrie was clearly disorganized as no one had come to investigate what had just happened inside the hangar.

"Jackrabbit, you have incoming. NATO has finally responded. You need to get out of there as soon as possible."

He dismissed the idea as he eyed the launcher sitting nearby. "Negative, Control. I need an expert on this launcher on the other end of these comms, and I mean now. I think I might have the launch codes here which means I might have the abort codes."

"Say again, Jackrabbit?"

"Get me an expert, now!"

"Stand by, Jackrabbit."

Jack stopped at the edge of the open door and peered around the corner. "Skylark, Jackrabbit. Do you read?"

Sherrie replied immediately. "I read you, Jackrabbit."

"Do you have video or static image transmission capability?"

"I do."

"Then get your ass over here. I have pages I might need to send to Langley."

"On my way."

Sherrie's countdown hit zero but she held off firing her next round, not wanting to give away her position now that she had a more critical task. Valkyrie's response to each volley was getting more coordinated, despite the fact hundreds had already abandoned their posts. It meant each time they fired, the snipers defending the base against her fire teams opened up all the more quickly.

Shots rang out all around her, single shots, the disciplined assault continuing for over twenty minutes now. The Valkyrie response was immediate, heavy gunfire lasting less than ten seconds before falling silent.

She rose, rushing through the stalks, yelling at the top of her lungs. "All teams, fire at will!"

Gunfire responded all around her as she emerged from the wheat and sprinted through the weeds. She kept her head down but her rifle ready as she neared the fence line, watching for any Valkyrie asshole who might spot her. Someone poked their head up and she took him out with two rounds then slung her rifle, leaping at the fence and swinging over the top, dropping to the other side as bullets tore at the barbed wire she had barely cleared.

Her fire teams responded, pouring lead on the area as she crawled on her belly for cover. Valkyrie continued to flee the battle, more of their trucks racing away as she pressed her back against a building near the fence line. "Time to first impact?"

"You've got five minutes," replied Leroux.

"Time to missile reaching target?"

"Three."

"Then no time to waste." She pushed to her feet. "Guide me in."

Jack raised his AK-47, slowly scanning left to right for the enemy. He spotted a couple of dozen, but they were all retreating to the main gate, nobody paying any attention to him. If he were to open fire, it would defeat the purpose, merely drawing attention to himself.

He jogged toward the launcher, his head on a swivel, hoping to simply blend in if anyone glanced in his direction, since he was wearing Valkyrie gear. He reached the launcher and slung his assault rifle, placing his pistol on a foothold, where he could easily reach it.

"Control, I'm at the launcher."

A subject matter expert responded. "There should be a shield covering the panel. Do you see it?"

Jack was already standing in front of the panel he had seen Chekalov working on earlier. "Yes, there's a key in the bottom right."

"Turn it counterclockwise then lift. It should raise the entire cover. That will give you access."

Jack twisted the key and gently lifted the cover, revealing the control panel, the display showing the missile's position, chilling. "I've got access."

"The launch code should be displayed at the top. It's a ten-digit alphanumeric code."

Jack eyed the panel, the code obvious. "Got it."

"See if you can find that in your list of launch codes."

Jack flipped through the book, each page with handwritten codes and GPS coordinates. "Got it."

"Is there another code on the page, ten digits?"

He smiled. "Affirmative."

"Okay, that should be the abort code. Now listen carefully, press—"

Two shots rang out and Jack gasped as he was hit in the back, slamming him against the panel before he collapsed, his world a sea of pain and blackness.

I guess we all die.

Sherrie suppressed the urge to cry out as Jack got shot in the back. She raised her weapon and took out the shooter.

"Hold up!" came Leroux's voice in her ear.

She froze.

"Two hostiles approaching your position, around the corner to your right."

She waited, the footfalls growing louder. They came into sight, sprinting toward the main gate, and she held her fire, not wanting to draw any more attention to herself or Jack.

"You're clear."

She sprinted to Jack's side, blood oozing from two wounds in his back. She checked for a pulse but found none. She repositioned her fingers.

"Skylark, forget him. You have to deactivate the missile."

"But I might be able to save him."

"It's him or millions."

She cursed and grabbed the black book still clutched in Jack's hand. "What do I do?" She listened to a voice she didn't recognize on the other end, pressing several keys while watching her back, then entered a code.

The panel flashed red, displaying an error message.

"It didn't work!"

Something grabbed her calf and she drew her sidearm from its holster, aiming it at her target. It was Jack.

"Reverse the code."

"What?"

"Look at the pattern." He collapsed. "Reverse the code."

She stared at the failed abort code.

"Skylark, whatever you're going to do, make it quick. You've got two minutes before the first cruise missiles hit and less than sixty seconds before nuclear detonation."

"I'm reversing the code." She reentered the sequence of commands then the reversed code and hit Enter. The panel beeped, a message appearing indicating a self-destruct command had been transmitted.

"Skylark, what's your status?"

"It says it's been transmitted. Can you see if it's detonated?"

"Stand by, Skylark."

"There's no time for that." She reached down and grabbed Jack, hauling him to his feet. He gasped as she lifted him with a fireman's carry.

"You've got sixty seconds, Skylark. Get the hell out of there! There's nothing you can do now!"

"You don't have to ask me twice." She rushed towards the fence line, eying the sky to the west, cursing at the contrails streaking across the sky.

"Control Actual, Skylark…" Her voice caught in her throat. This was no time for callsigns. "Sweetheart, I don't think we're going to make it. I love you. Don't ever forget that."

The anguish in Leroux's reply broke her heart. "I love you, too. Just keep running. Don't give up."

A flash on the horizon to the south had her heart skipping a beat. "I just saw a detonation."

Jubilation filled her ear. "You did it, hon! You did it! The missile detonated. Non-nuclear. You saved them. You saved us all."

The sound of a cruise missile screeching toward her had her cringing as the warhead slammed into the ground behind her, blasting her off her feet.

Goodbye, my love.

Operations Center 3, CIA Headquarters

Langley, Virginia

Leroux watched in horror as missile after missile hammered the base, fireballs erupting as the entire facility was leveled.

Tong turned, her voice subdued. "We just lost comms with Jackrabbit and Skylark."

Leroux collapsed into his chair and Morrison squeezed his shoulder, taking over as Leroux's heart broke. "Keep trying," instructed Morrison. "And analyze the footage of the fence line. If she made it far enough, she might just make it."

Leroux sniffed hard and opened his eyes as his team sprang into action.

And Tong cried out. "I've got her!"

465th Missile Brigade

Yuzhny Military Base, Belarus

Sherrie pushed to her feet, Jack still over her shoulder, her leg muscles screaming as she struggled to lift him. "You better still be alive back there."

He squeezed her ass but said nothing.

"I'll take that as a yes. Hold on, buddy. We're almost there."

Impact after impact continued to shake the ground, but she was only feet from the fence line now and the targets were the buildings placed at least thirty yards from the perimeter. It didn't mean she was safe, not by a long shot. Shrapnel, a missile slightly off-target, anything, could still rip them apart.

She reached the fence and found several Belarusians there, a hole cut. They helped her through, two of them taking charge of Jack as they fell back from the base several hundred yards, well away from any potential shrapnel. Jack was lowered to the ground and a medic rushed over, setting to work. He removed Jack's flak jacket and she sighed in relief to see the two rounds to the back still visible, though deep..

"He should be fine."

One of the men who had helped rescue them raised his weapon. "He's wearing Valkyrie gear. Is he—"

Sherrie cut him off. "He's FSB. Like me, he was undercover. Patch him up and get me a ride. Our job isn't finished."

The medic looked up at her. "Your job might not be finished, but his is."

Operations Center 3, CIA Headquarters

Langley, Virginia

Leroux stood in stunned silence, still recovering from the roller coaster of emotions he had experienced over the past five minutes. Valkyrie had successfully launched a nuke toward Ukraine. Whether it was meant for an air burst or a ground detonation didn't matter. It was the first hostile deployment of a nuke since World War II, and the only ever hostile missile launch. Jack and Sherrie had managed to abort the missile just in time, but that wasn't what had him so shaken. It was the fact that for a brief moment, he thought the most important person in his life, the only woman he had ever loved and the only woman he ever intended to love, was dead.

But she wasn't.

Thank God.

A portion of the satellite feed isolated in the bottom right of the massive display arcing across the front of the room showed Sherrie and

Jack with a group of Belarusian soldiers, well back from the now decimated base. She was safe. They were safe.

For the moment.

Tong turned in her chair. "We've got a flash from the Pentagon. The Russian forces that have been mobilizing along the Belarusian border are moving."

Morrison cursed. "How long before they reach the border?"

"Pentagon estimates as little as twenty minutes."

"Have the Belarusians responded?"

"Not yet. They probably don't know. Right now, they think we're attacking them."

Child grunted. "We are. We've destroyed all their missile sites. Their time as a nuclear power is over."

Leroux agreed and turned to Tong. "When did the Russians make their move?"

She checked the report. "Within about five minutes of when the first missile should have detonated."

Leroux's eyes narrowed and he turned to Morrison. "Do they not know? They should by now."

"Their military definitely knows. But if this was a secret plan hatched between their president and Pikalov, they might be trying to figure out what's going on."

Leroux tapped his chin. "They're not in on the plan."

Morrison regarded him. "Someone issued the order to go."

"Yes. But the fact they did tells me they don't know the operation has failed."

Morrison grabbed the phone once again. "We need to make sure they know. There's still time to stop this and save Belarus."

465th Missile Brigade

Yuzhny Military Base, Belarus

Sherrie kept a comforting hand on Jack's leg as she surveyed the area, the bombardment of the base slowing as NATO commanders reviewed satellite footage for bomb damage assessment. From her viewpoint, it was flattened, and in retrospect, she was thankful the Belarusian forces had fled otherwise they would have been massacred along with the Valkyrie forces who had stood their ground.

The Belarusian medic working on Jack turned to her. "He needs more medical attention than I can provide. He's got cracked ribs and might have internal bleeding. We need to evac him to a hospital. There's no way you can just load him in the back of a car and continue your mission."

She pointed at a nearby jeep, several of which had pulled up in the past few minutes. "Get him in the back. I'll take him."

A Belarusian colonel emerged from the tall wheat stalks and eyed the woman giving orders. "Who the hell are you?"

"I'm Special Agent Abisov, FSB."

"Bullshit. Show me some ID."

"I'm undercover. Do you seriously think I carry FSB ID?"

The captain from her first encounter stepped forward. "Sir, I can't speak as to whether she is who she claims to be, but I can tell you if it weren't for her, we would've lost the day. She's the one who organized the counterattack, came up with a plan, and kept us all going."

The colonel regarded her then turned to the captain. "I don't know if that says more about you than her. This base should have never been lost."

A massive explosion rocked the area, a fireball roiling into the sky as the fuel reserves ignited, sending the last remaining of the Valkyrie invaders scrambling into their transports and heading back to their base.

The colonel growled in frustration. "I don't have time for this. Arrest them both. We'll sort this out later. Right now, we've got more important things to deal with."

"What's that?" asked Sherrie.

He pointed to the west. "We're at war with NATO."

Operations Center 3, CIA Headquarters

Langley, Virginia

Leroux watched with the others and he couldn't help but smile slightly, many on his team grinning broadly, as the frustration of the past several days was taken out on the Valkyrie forces responsible for so much chaos. NATO was delivering justice, finally having taken action the moment the missile had launched, the moment there was a provocation they could no longer ignore. And at the moment, Valkyrie's shiny new base, capable of holding 15,000 troops comfortably, along with their retreating column of personnel forced out of the Belarusian missile base by Sherrie and her counterattack, were being decimated by NATO airstrikes.

The screen was split, the left showing the base, the right showing the column, as bombs and missiles launched from ships, planes, and the ground repeatedly hammered the road the retreating Valkyrie forces were on, and the base where 7,000 of their comrades were caught flatfooted. It was a slaughter, but the bastards deserved it. This organization was responsible for countless deaths, certainly in the thousands if not tens of thousands. The more damage that could be done to them now, under the guise of punishing Belarus for launching a nuke, the better.

If they killed 8,000 of them today, that was 8,000 fewer the world would have to deal with tomorrow, for he feared this wasn't the end of the paramilitary organization, backed and funded by Russia and its out-of-control president. Valkyrie would be a force that would terrorize the world for years to come, though perhaps not as much as they might have fifteen minutes ago.

He turned to Tong. "What are the Russians doing?"

"They're still advancing toward the border. Wait a minute. Holy shit! They're launching!"

She tapped at her keyboard and brought up the latest feed from the Pentagon, and everyone watched in horror as a map appeared showing hundreds of missiles tracking from within Russia, all heading into Belarus.

Leroux snapped his fingers at the room. "Are any of those heading for our people?"

Tong shook her head. "Too early to tell, but it's a safe bet. It looks like they're gonna hit everything."

Leroux activated the comms. "Skylark, Jackrabbit, this is Control Actual. The Russians have launched. You've got hundreds of missiles inbound. We're attempting to track, but you may have incoming, over."

En Route to Babruysk Air Base, Belarus

Jack lay flat on his stomach on an incredibly uncomfortable stretcher, unable to acknowledge or act upon Leroux's latest warning about inbound Russian missiles.. His back was killing him and he was having difficulty breathing. Each breath was a shot of agony. He definitely had cracked or broken ribs, which would take him out of the game for a while, and that pissed him off. The medic continued to monitor his vitals, but Jack already knew he was fine. He might have internal bleeding, but he doubted it. If it was, it wouldn't be anything serious.

He had caught both rounds to his upper back, the flak jacket limiting the damage. The medic had removed the bullets, indicating to him how deeply they had penetrated, which wasn't far. Nothing had made it past the rib cage. His heart was fine, his lungs were fine, and the bullets had come nowhere near any other vital organs. He would live, though it would take him weeks to recover, depending on how badly cracked his ribs were. But he was alive for the moment and so was Sherrie, who sat across from him, handcuffed.

They hadn't bothered cuffing him due to his condition, which was a mistake on their part, and right now, he debated what he should do. There was one medic and one guard in the back. There was a driver and another guard in the front. But other than that, he had no idea what lay beyond their ambulance.

His comms squawked in his ear. "Jackrabbit and Skylark, this is Control Actual. Delta is still inbound. They'll be inserted near wherever you end up, but they won't have a ride home. They'll attempt a rescue, then you guys will have to get across the border on your own. Unfortunately, that's the best we can do at the moment, but we're working on a better plan. Just sit tight. Delta is on their way, over."

Jack wanted to tell them to abort, but he couldn't without revealing the fact he had comms. He turned his head slightly and exchanged a look with Sherrie, who had also heard the report. She shook her head slightly, indicating for him not to act. From where she sat, she could see out the rear window, but also through the front, the hatch open between the driver cab and the back where he lay. She had far more situational awareness than he did, and if she were indicating for him not to do anything stupid, there had to be a reason for it. He had no idea what she was seeing outside those windows. For all he knew, there could be half a dozen escorts, so even if they escaped the ambulance, they would be gunned down the moment they opened the doors.

The driver shouted from the front. "We're at the base!"

Jack frowned.

Decision made.

En Route to Babruysk Air Base, Belarus

"You boys might wanna see this."

Dawson rose and poked his head into the cockpit as the others peered through the side windows of the Black Hawk helicopter carrying them deeper into Belarusian territory. The sun was low on the horizon behind them, the view ahead dark, lit up by explosions, some close by, some far off in the distance as NATO took out Belarusian military targets, and from the east, Russia hit anything they wanted.

It was a satisfying sight in some ways. The Belarusians had gone to bed with the wrong partner, had allied themselves with evil, and the destruction of their military was a suitable punishment. But unfortunately, with the Russians now attacking, that meant not only were military targets being hit, but likely infrastructure and even civilian targets like they continued to do in Ukraine. The Russians didn't care about the rules of war. They were little better than terrorists. Killing innocents didn't register with them, though he did give them more credit than terrorist scum.

The average Russian soldier wasn't a bad person. He was just led by bad people. Terrorists, hell-bent on the slaughter of millions, were rotten to the core, every one of them evil, every one of them thinking of their enemy as insects, not as human beings. There could be no peace with people like that, nor those who supported them.

The disgusting thing was that people weren't born with hatred. It was taught, it was the adults that taught their children to hate, and it was their grandparents that had taught them. But there was no exclusive hold on hate. Even America, the country he was proud to put his life on the line for every day, was filled with learned hate, whether that was whites hating blacks, blacks hating whites, Republicans hating Democrats, or straights hating homosexuals. It was all learned, all taught.

He peered out the cockpit window at a country being destroyed, its people taught to hate the West, to hate anything different than themselves, and it broke his heart. Every soldier swore to protect his country, but none wanted war. If he could snap his fingers and end all the bigotry, the racism, the hatred, the discrimination, and turn his weapons into plowshares, he would. Unfortunately, this was a world built on hate, and he could see no solution to the problem, not when the greatest country in the world hated itself.

If America couldn't succeed where the rest of the world had failed, what hope was there?

He sighed. Maggie wanted kids, and so did he, but to bring them into this world where neighbor hated neighbor, where family couldn't even get together at Thanksgiving without violent arguments breaking out? Did he want to bring a child into a world like that?

Niner poked his head up beside him. "Something bothering you, BD?"

"No more than usual."

Niner stared out ahead. "It'd be almost beautiful if every one of those explosions didn't mean someone was dying."

Dawson grunted. "You're right."

Niner pursed his lips. "Here's a question. What does it mean if NATO and Russia are both attacking Belarus? Are we allies or mutual enemies?"

Dawson returned to his seat. "No idea. Philosophy would tell us, the enemy of my enemy is my friend, but right now, everyone's our enemy. Russians, Belarusians, Valkyrie. Right now, inside this country, we only have two friends and they're in the middle of this shit."

Babruysk Air Base, Belarus

Jack lay on a table in a rather ordinary procedure room, painted all white. It was clean, but it was sparse. It wasn't like something back home filled with machines and computers and every other device you could think of. Here, there was a procedure tray, a nurse, a doctor, Sherrie sitting in the corner cuffed, and two guards with their weapons at the ready by the door.

Jack winced as yet another stitch was put in.

The doctor shook his head. "I don't know why you won't let me give you an anesthetic."

"The pain lets me know I'm alive."

The doctor grunted. "So does the fact you can see and hear."

Jack shrugged then winced, and the doctor admonished him.

"You're going to have to take it easy or you're going to tear your stitches. Now stay still, I've got one last one to put in."

He braced himself and the needle pierced his skin, exiting the other side of the wound a moment later. He felt the tug then the knot being tied, then heard the snip of the scissors.

The doctor stepped back. "There you go, you're all stitched up. You're going to hurt for a while, but you'll live. Take some ibuprofen for the pain as needed and try to take it easy for a couple of weeks. You'll be back to your normal self soon enough and back serving whoever you call master."

Jack rolled onto his side and jerked his chin at the guards. "Don't tell me you believe their master's bullshit that we aren't who we say we are."

The doctor snapped off his rubber gloves, tossing them into a nearby waste bin. "Not my job to even care about that shit. I treat you whether you're friend or foe."

Jack grinned. "I'd like to be your friend, Doc."

The man laughed. "If only it were that easy."

Sirens wailed and the doctor cursed.

"What is it?" asked Jack.

"That's an air raid siren. Something tells me we're at war, so my advice to take it easy might not be possible." The doctor left the room with the nurse and Jack stood, gently stretching.

Sherrie gave him a look. "Careful, you don't want to tear your stitches like he said."

The sirens continued to wail and Jack turned his back toward the guards and bent over, his gown untied, revealing his ass and balls to their captors. Both groaned and turned away in disgust as Sherrie slipped out of her cuffs. She grabbed the sidearm of the closest soldier, putting two rounds in his head then his partner as Jack lost the robe and faced her on full display.

"Who's my size?"

She gestured at Jack Jr. "Not many."

He grinned. "Get your mind outta the gutter, juicy buns. I meant uniform."

She pointed at the first guard. "Him. That's why I shot him in the head."

Jack flashed her a smile. "So thoughtful." He took a knee and began stripping the man out of his uniform as Sherrie checked the hallway, sounds of panic outside. He quickly dressed, finding the uniform a reasonable fit, at least enough that it should fool anyone rushing past them. "I'm ready. Let's get the hell out of here."

Sherrie activated her comms. "Control, Skylark. Where's that ride?"

En Route to Babruysk Air Base, Belarus

The Black Hawk thundered toward their destination, almost skimming the trees as the pilot hugged the deck, avoiding enemy radar. Explosions continued on the horizon in all directions as NATO and Russia pounded Belarus. Dawson wasn't overly concerned about most of the targets. What did concern him was anti-aircraft installations. The more of those that were taken out, the safer their ride would be.

The pilot pointed ahead. "That's our LZ. It's less than five miles from the base."

"Copy that." Dawson turned to the others. "Equipment check." Everyone began inspecting their equipment and those of their partner as his comms squawked.

"Zero-One, Control. Jackrabbit and Skylark have freed themselves. They're on their way to you now, over."

"Control, Zero-One. Understood, over." He leaned back into the cockpit. "Our targets are on the way. Can you hold?"

The pilot guided them into the LZ and they bounced onto the ground, Dawson's team exiting the chopper and rapidly heading for the tree line of the small clearing. "Those aren't my orders, Sergeant Major, but oddly enough, I'm experiencing some technical difficulties. I'm probably not gonna be able to take off for ten, maybe fifteen minutes."

Dawson grinned, slapping the man on the shoulder. "I like how you think."

Babruysk Air Base, Belarus

Jack, in a Belarusian uniform, armed with a Makarov pistol on his hip and an AK-47 gripped in his hands, strode swiftly down the corridor with Sherrie at his side. An explosion rocked the base, shouts of panic and alarm surrounded them. They were in a hospital with a lot of civilians and a mostly female nursing contingent. This wasn't like the Valkyrie base where it was nothing but battle-hardened troops. It was quite likely there wasn't a single person here who had ever been shot at.

Panic would be the order of the day.

They reached the doors as another impact was felt, followed quickly by two more. He pushed open the doors and stepped out into the evening air, his nostrils filling with the smell of burning wood as flames flickered up into the sky, drowning out the stars overhead that had just begun appearing. An ambulance idled nearby, its crew cowering behind it. Jack opened the passenger side door and climbed in as Sherrie slid across the hood and occupied the driver's seat. She put it in gear and pulled away, its crew shouting after them then calling for help.

Sherrie activated her comms. "Control, Skylark. How the hell do I get out of here?"

Jack rolled down his window, prepping his weapon in case he had to fire as Leroux guided them toward the main gate as missile after missile slammed into the installation, rapidly leveling it.

"There's the gate," said Sherrie, pointing ahead. Jack leaned forward, glancing in the side mirror to confirm no one was pursuing them. It was clear. Sherrie blasted through the gate, stunning the guards, and it took them a few moments before they opened fire. She swerved left to right, not providing them with an easy target, then rounded a bend, putting a thatch of trees between them and those firing upon them. She grinned at Jack. "Looks like we got out just in time."

"Looks that way." He tapped his ear. "Control, Jackrabbit, please tell us our ride is still here, over."

"Confirmed, Jackrabbit. You're five minutes out. Stay on the road you're on and we'll guide you in, over."

"Copy that, Control."

Sherrie cursed and Jack looked at her. "What?"

She jerked her head toward her side mirror. "We've got company."

Jack checked his own and growled in frustration at the sight of two light armored vehicles giving chase. "We're not out of this yet."

Outside Babruysk Air Base, Belarus

Dawson took a knee amidst his men holding at the tree line, the massive Black Hawk behind them idling, its rotors slowly turning, quiet enough that it shouldn't attract any attention, not with the assault on the nearest military facility barely five miles from here still underway.

His comms squawked. "Zero-One, Control. They've cleared the gate and they're en route to your position, two LAVs pursuing them, over."

"Copy that, Control. Heading to the rendezvous now." Dawson rose and swirled his hand over his head, the pilot giving a thumbs-up. "Let's go save the CIA's ass once again!" he said, heading into the trees toward the road less than half a mile away.

"I've always wondered how that worked," said Niner as they pushed through the undergrowth.

"What's that?" asked Atlas, his impossibly deep voice sending a flock of birds away in terror.

"Does the Pentagon send Langley a bill?"

"I think it's all one wallet."

"It is, but everybody has their own budgets. If this little outing costs a million bucks, and its purpose is to retrieve two CIA people, I'm sure the Pentagon would like that million bucks back in their budget so they could spend it on something else."

"I think you're forgetting this is our job, little man."

Niner shrugged. "I suppose it is. The only time Langley will ever get a bill for our services is if we go private."

Jimmy grinned. "I hear Valkyrie's hiring. They suddenly have eight thousand openings."

Spock cocked an eyebrow. "You'd consider going private?"

Niner shook his head. "Not as long as Uncle Sam will have me. He's the best employer ever," sighed the Korean-American warrior wistfully.

Snickers from the team had Dawson smiling. If he went private, he could make a fortune. Command sergeant majors were in high demand, especially ex-Special Forces, but he loved his job and he loved serving his country. Going private usually meant serving someone else, some civilian he might not respect, some corporation whose policies he might not support. In this job, in this army, he knew whom he served.—the president, the constitution, the flag, the citizens, all of whom he would die for.

Engines roaring had Dawson raising a fist, ending the conversation. He cocked an ear. They were coming from their right. He pressed forward, reaching the edge of the road. "Prep the eighty-four," he told Atlas, who unslung the Carl Gustaf 84mm recoilless rifle and loaded it.

"There they are," said Niner, pointing.

An ambulance careened around the corner, barely keeping all four wheels on the pavement, two light armored vehicles in pursuit.

"Atlas, target the middle vehicle. The rest of you, the rear."

Atlas took aim. "Firing! Firing! Firing!" He squeezed the trigger, the distinctive pop of the rifle drowned out by M4s opening up on full auto, the armor-piercing rounds making quick work of the engine compartment of the rear vehicle. The nearest LAV exploded in a brilliant flash of orange and yellow, the wreckage careening off the road and flipping onto its side.

Dawson continued to fire on the other LAV as it ground to a halt, the occupants throwing open their doors and returning fire, quickly mowed down. "Hold your fire!" he ordered.

As the ambulance came to a halt, Sherrie hopped out and pointed to the passenger side. "Jack needs help. He's been shot in the back twice."

Dawson cursed and directed Niner and Jimmy to the opposite side of the ambulance as Spock and Atlas covered their sixes. "Report."

"He was shot at the base while disarming the weapon. He's been treated and stitched up but I think in all the excitement he's torn his stitches."

Dawson peered into the cab to see Jack gingerly stepping out, blood soaking the seat. "Yeah, he definitely tore his stitches."

Jimmy and Niner formed a human chair and they fell back toward the chopper, its rotors now thundering. There would be no hiding their ride if anyone else came looking.

Gunfire rattled from behind the rear trailing LAV, somebody obviously having survived. Dawson and Spock laid down cover fire as

Jack was carried into the tree line. Atlas fired another round from the Carl Gustaf, putting a quick end to the Belarusian attempt to retrieve their prisoner.

Dawson rose, listening before announcing the all-clear. "Let's get the hell out of here before somebody comes looking to see what all these explosions are."

"Get to the chopper!" yelled Niner, and Sherrie gave him a look.

"Maybe if Atlas did it, it'd be more believable. Your impression of Ahhnold is too girly."

Niner eyed her. "As if you could do better."

"Get to the chopper!"

His eyes shot wide at her far better impression. "How the hell did you do that?"

She shrugged. "I guess my balls have already dropped."

Everyone roared in laughter at Niner's expense as they broke into the clearing and boarded the chopper.

Dawson poked his head into the cockpit, the last boot to clear the ground. "Let's get the hell out of here. Somebody's gonna come looking for their friends."

"You got it, Sergeant Major. Everybody, hold on. This could be a bumpy ride."

Operations Center 3, CIA Headquarters

Langley, Virginia

Cheers erupted as the chopper lifted off and banked hard to the left, heading west and back toward NATO territory. Hugs and high-fives were the order of the day, and Leroux adjusted his headset as Dawson reported their status.

"Control, Zero-One. We have the targets and are heading home, over."

"Copy that, Zero-One. Status on the targets?"

"Skylark is intact. Jackrabbit has two open wounds on his back. He's being tended to now. He'll survive."

"Copy that, Zero-One. NATO forces will provide cover for your extraction, but note that all other hostilities by our side have halted."

"Copy that, Control. And the Russians?"

Leroux checked the tactical display, the feed from the Pentagon showing the Russian units still advancing. "They're about to reach the border. At this moment, it looks like we might be about to lose Belarus to the Russians."

"Understood, Control. Zero-One, out."

Leroux gripped the back of his chair as he stood behind it, staring at the indicator showing the chopper, deep in Belarusian territory, slowly making its way westward as a NATO fighter escort closed in on their position.

The doors to the operations center hissed open and Morrison entered, the room immediately settling down. He cocked an eyebrow at everyone. "Aren't I the killjoy."

Leroux waved a hand at the displays. "Sorry, sir. We were just celebrating. Bravo Team has recovered Jack and Sherrie. Their chopper is in the air now."

"ETA to the border?"

Leroux glanced over at Tong who checked her station. "Thirty minutes." She cursed and tapped at her station, the immediate airspace around the chopper suddenly filling the entire display. "We've got inbound."

Leroux stared at the screen, his eyes taking in the various indicators and cursed at the sight of two Belarusian MiG-29s closing in on the chopper.

En Route to Polish Airspace, Belarus

The pilot cursed. "We've got inbound, two MiGs."

Jack, still in pain, watched as Dawson rushed forward. "Have they fired yet?"

"Negative. I'm hugging the tree line but they've got us. They're probably just waiting for orders."

Jack pushed to his feet, groaning loudly, and Dawson turned.

"Sit down before you get yourself killed."

Jack gave him a look. "It sounds like you're about to get us all killed anyway." He reached forward. "Give me a headset."

The copilot handed one back and Jack fit it in place. "Put me on with them."

A switch was flipped. "You're on."

Jack spoke Russian, a language all Belarusian pilots would speak. "This is FSB Ghost Flight Alpha Four to inbound MiGs. Break off your approach immediately. You're interfering with an important mission, over."

There was no reply.

Jack glanced over his shoulder at the others. "Can you believe they're ignoring me?"

"I would," replied Niner.

"So would I," rumbled Atlas.

"Oh, ye of little faith." Jack removed his hand from the mic. "I repeat. This is FSB Ghost Flight Alpha Four to approaching MiGs. Break off your approach immediately, over."

"Negative, FSB helicopter. You are ordered to turn around and land at Babruysk Air Base immediately. Comply or you will be destroyed. Acknowledge, over."

"Negative. We are on a priority FSB mission, and just in case you've forgotten, FSB is Russian intelligence."

The pilot cursed in Belarusian. "We're now at war with you bastards. Your mission is not in the Belarusian interest. My orders are to shoot you down if you do not comply. Turn around now or I will execute my orders!"

Jack relaxed his voice, recognizing the tension in the pilot's. "Listen, I know we're at war, but we shouldn't be. I need to finish my mission so I can inform Moscow what has really happened here, so this war can stop before it gets going."

"I have no way to confirm that."

"No, you don't. But I'll ask you this. We are one chopper. How important can we be compared to the possibility I'm telling the truth? If

I'm lying, then all that happens is a chopper with a few people on it got away. If I'm telling the truth, it might stop Russia from taking over your country, perhaps killing thousands or more during the attack. What do you want to do?"

There was a pause and everyone waited with bated breath, those who spoke Russian translating for the others.

"Good luck, FSB Ghost Flight Alpha Four."

Jack's comms in his ears squawked. "Jackrabbit, Control. They're breaking off!"

The pilot confirmed it a moment later. "They're breaking off. Holy shit, buddy, whatever you said worked!"

Atlas slapped Jack on the back. "You're one smooth talker."

Jack gasped in pain, collapsing to his knees.

"Oh, shit. Sorry, dude, I forgot."

Jack handed the headset back to the copilot then Atlas helped him back into his seat. Jack leaned back, letting the pain subside, then gave Atlas the stink eye. "The next time someone on this team wants to thank me, send someone smaller." He pointed at Niner. "Like him."

Niner gave him the bird. "Trust me, I can hurt you."

Jack eyeballed him. "You keep thinking that, snuggle bunny."

Operations Center 3, CIA Headquarters

Langley, Virginia

Tong's thumb thrust into the air. "It's confirmed! They've crossed the border!"

More cheers broke out as Leroux collapsed into his chair, relief spreading through his body like a wave. Sherrie was safe, but this wasn't over yet. The two people he was responsible for, plus the team sent to rescue them that was under his command, were now safe, but the prospect of war still loomed. They had foiled the attempt at removing Kyiv from the map, but the other part of the plan, to use the nuclear launch as an excuse to take over Belarus, was still underway. It could mean the spreading of the war now underway in Europe along an even longer stretch of NATO's border.

Tong thrust two arms in the air, spinning toward him. "The Russians have halted their launches!"

Everyone stopped and stared at the screens, the latest tactical display from the Pentagon showing no more missiles being tracked from

Russian territory, the only ones still on the screen already in Belarusian territory.

"What about their ground forces?"

She returned to her seat. "No change."

"Poor communications?" asked Packman.

Leroux frowned. "Anything's possible."

They continued to watch the Russian ground forces close in on the border, the first units about to breach at any moment.

"Zoom in on the closest unit."

"Yes, sir." Tong worked her keyboard and the satellite image appeared, showing a column of tanks and support vehicles racing along a road, a border checkpoint on the left side of the screen.

"They can't be more than a mile," muttered Child, his customary spin forgotten.

There was a squawk and a priority alert from the Pentagon appeared. Tong tapped her keyboard and the main display was replaced with the text of the update.

Russian forces on Belarus border ordered to stand down.

There were more cheers and Leroux rose along with Tong. He stepped over and gave her a one-armed hug then returned his attention to the screen as she cleared the Pentagon flash.

The tanks still raced forward.

"Why aren't they stopping?" asked Child, desperation in his voice. "Why doesn't somebody tell them to stop?"

The celebration halted. Leroux stared at the satellite feed, the column of tanks continuing to race forward, diesel fumes spewing from their exhausts obscuring their approach on the overhead satellite. He closed his eyes.

Please, God, please.

"They're stopping!"

He smiled.

Thank you.

He opened his eyes to see the column of tanks coming to an abrupt halt less than a hundred yards shy of the border. But were they stopping because they had been ordered to, or were they preparing to fire before crossing? "Is there any sign they're exchanging fire?"

He glanced around the room, everyone shaking their head.

"Look," said Child, pointing.

Leroux spun to see the tanks turning around. His shoulders slumped in relief and he dropped back into his chair, smiling at Tong. "I don't think I've ever been so tense in my life."

"Me neither," she agreed. "I just can't wait to see how the Kremlin spins this one."

Leroux laughed. "My bet is they'll deny it happened and blame NATO for all the attacks."

She extended a hand. "I'll take that bet."

Sheremetyevo Airport

Moscow, Russia

Exactly Two Months After Taking of Rostov-on-Don

Jack stretched, still a little stiff from taking two rounds in the back a couple of months ago, but he was almost fully recovered. He had already been cleared for active duty, and this was his first op since being benched. It was one anyone could have done, but the Chief had agreed to give him first crack at it. It was a loose end that had to be tied up, and he wanted the job.

He had earned it.

Things had settled down. Valkyrie's presence in Europe was mostly wiped out, though there were still thousands of personnel at various other interests in the world. The war in Ukraine continued as it had, most not realizing how close they had come to annihilation. The Russian troops had pulled back from the Belarusian border, many redeploying south to fill the gap left by the annihilation of the Valkyrie contingent.

The Belarusians were pissed at everyone. They had been bombed by both sides. All Russian troops had been ordered out of the country and NATO was offering to help rebuild, the peace overture being received well in Minsk, though decried by a Moscow screaming bloody murder if Belarus realigned with the West.

The Ukrainians were using the entire fiasco as an example of why Russia had to be stopped. And as predicted, the Russian press was making no mention of anything, the people of Russia mostly left in the dark as to how close the world had come to nuclear war, even if only on a limited scale.

The Valkyrie base had been obliterated, and what remained of their forces were either integrating with the Russian military, disappearing into the woodwork, or heading for operations in Africa.

And Pikalov was still a free man, which was a minor miracle. Failure usually wasn't tolerated in Russia, and it had him wondering if Pikalov had something on the Russian president, something compromising, something that if made known, would bring him down.

But none of that mattered.

A baggage handler approached, his patch indicating he worked at Sheremetyevo Airport. The man smiled as Jack pushed off the wall he was leaning against. "Did you get my gift on board?"

"Yes, sir."

Jack smiled. "Perfect." He handed the man an envelope, chock full of cash. "I was never here."

The man opened the envelope and did a quick flip through the money before pocketing his payday. "Neither was I."

En Route to St. Petersburg, Russia

Pikalov sat in an Embraer Legacy 600, one of the many planes owned by Valkyrie. They had taken massive losses, almost 8,000 men dead. In addition, in the immediate aftermath, the Russian Army had taken advantage of the chaos, forcing thousands more to sign contracts to enlist, taking them off the Valkyrie payroll. He had lost over half of his personnel, though none of his business interests. The fight in Ukraine was partially about money, but it was a temporary thing. The war would eventually end, as would the contracts to fight in it. He intended to build an empire. He intended to be a billionaire, and their mining interests in Africa were just the start.

The president was pissed. Everything had gone so right and then so wrong. Unfortunately, he had no clue what had actually happened. There had been a traitor in their midst, and they must be responsible for the failure. But who was it? All of his senior commanders were dead, and there were few survivors in Belarus. Those he had spoken to had seen nothing to explain what had happened to the nuke.

How could a plan fail after the successful launch of a nuclear weapon?

He had read the intelligence reports, which confirmed it had detonated on its own. It wasn't intercepted by the Ukrainians. Somebody had used the launcher to self-destruct the missile. Could it have been Chekalov? He refused to believe it. The man was incredibly loyal, and besides, why would he launch something then destroy it?

No, it couldn't have been him.

His satellite phone rang and he answered. "Hello?"

"Hey, General. It's Jack."

Pikalov's eyes shot wide and he leaned forward, genuinely excited. "Jack, you survived! Thank God! Where are you, my friend?"

"I'm in Moscow."

Pikalov's eyes narrowed. "Wait a minute. I just left there a few minutes ago." He tensed. There was no way that was a coincidence. "What's going on?"

"I was just delivering a gift."

Pikalov looked about the cabin, everyone oblivious to what was going on. "A gift? What kind of gift?"

"The kind of gift that ends friendships and delivers justice."

Pikalov bolted out of his chair. "Land immediately!"

Everyone turned toward him. "What?" asked his new second-in-command.

Pikalov pointed at the cockpit. "Tell the pilot to land immediately!"

"Yes, sir!" His second-in-command scrambled toward the cockpit as Pikalov sat back down and fastened his seatbelt.

"Allow me to help you get to the ground," said Jack.

There was a beep on the other end of the line then a deafening explosion tore at the fuselage. Pikalov dropped his phone as he grabbed the seat in front of him, wind howling through the cabin, a horrifying screech of metal on the port side having everyone spinning toward it as the wing ripped away.

Alarms sounded and the pilot said something over the speakers, barely heard over the scream of the passengers and the roaring engines. He fumbled for his seat belt, tightening it with a yank, then clutched the armrests as the plane spun faster and faster toward the ground. He spotted his phone at his feet, caught on the chair in front of him. He leaned down and grabbed it, pressing it against his ear.

"Are you there, you traitor?"

"I am."

"Who do you work for, the president?"

"No, asshole. I work for Uncle Sam, and he's got a message for you."

Pikalov pressed the phone tighter against his ear, the whining engines ear-piercing. "What's that?"

"You should have stayed a hot dog vendor. Burn in hell, motherfu—"

THE END

ACKNOWLEDGMENTS

While working on this book, I was undergoing a medical crisis, probably the most serious of my life. I was in a battle to preserve my sight. What I had thought was just a case of bad dry eye caused by my CPAP mask, turned out to be diabetic retinopathy, the neovascular glaucoma having my eye pressure at 48 rather than the preferred sub-21 reading.

I was going blind in my left eye.

Rapidly.

I had just finished my last book, putting off seeing the optometrist as I was convinced it was merely dry eye, and called the closest optometrist. I described the symptoms and was given an appointment for the next morning. Within five minutes of seeing the optometrist, I had an emergency referral to the Eye Institute. That afternoon I received a phone call and was in at 8:30am the next morning, where I underwent a flurry of tests, then verbal dumps of what was wrong, little of it registering.

I was in shock.

Later that day, I had injections in both eyes to help begin the process of breaking up the extra veins that had grown due to my diabetes, and within two weeks had an Ahmed Valve implanted in my left eye to relieve the pressure. It was a 2.5-hour procedure that was supposed to take 45-60 minutes, all performed while wide awake with no head restraint.

It was a terrifying experience, though the drugs took the edge off the urge to bolt.

Just the edge.

It's now been almost a month since that surgery, and I'm doing much better. My pressure is in the normal range, my vision has improved dramatically—I'm driving again!—and I'm hoping to make a full recovery to the point where a good set of glasses will make up any shortfall.

I'm not one to preach—I leave that to my characters—but if you're diabetic, or know someone who is, make sure you, or they, get their eyes tested annually. I had no problems with my eyes until the sudden onset that occurred. Little did I know that this horrific disease was wreaking havoc behind the scenes. A simple eye exam would have caught it, and the injections could have begun before things got worse.

And for those who fear the idea of injections, they're nothing. They freeze your eye with some drops, put a little device in to hold your eyes open (you can still blink, it just does nothing), then there's a little tap, and it's over. A couple of times I've felt a little sharp pain that lasts a split second. The device is removed and you're sent home—you can't drive until the next day. Don't avoid these injections because you fear them. There's nothing to them, and any discomfort lasts a nanosecond.

Well worth it.

As usual, there are people to thank. Brent Richards for some weapons info, Ian Kennedy for some explosives info, my dad for all the research, and, as always, my wife, daughter, my late mother who will always be an angel on my shoulder as I write, as well as my friends for their continued support, and my fantastic proofreading team!

To those who have not already done so, please visit my website at www.jrobertkennedy.com, then sign up for the Insider's Club to be notified of new book releases. Your email address will never be shared or sold.

Thank you once again for reading.

Printed in the USA
CPSIA information can be obtained
at www.ICGtesting.com
LVHW090905230124
769552LV00008B/316/J